ROCK, ROLL, AND DIE

ROCK, ROLL, AND DIE

WILLIAM MALTESE

WILDSIDE PRESS

Chase Knightly of the rock-and-roll youradionetwork.com
and its affiliate WZ13 radio for having hosted my co-host,
Joanne JoJo Crockett, and my rock-music filled
NO BOUNDARIES RADIO SHOW.

Published by Wildside Press LLC.
www.wildsidebooks.com

CHAPTER ONE

Beynor Wilden was a pro and acted accordingly from beginning to end.

"Why don't you go take a shower if you'd like," David Stoff suggested, too tired at the finish to shower first.

Beynor got up from the bed. Looking down, he reached to let his fingers gently brush David's flushed cheek.

"It was good?" Beynor asked.

David doubted it had been all that good for Beynor, no matter how good … and it *had* been good … it had been for David. However, Beynor had proved himself more than just some ordinary hustler who hopped into bed and performed like a machine. David was well aware that Steven Gladson could get plenty of machine-like sex; if David was going to entice *that* bastard, as David planned, it was going to have to be with a hustler who was above the ordinary.

David watched Beynor walk bare-assed to the bathroom and shut the door behind him. Again, he reflected upon his good luck in finding someone who so nearly matched those characteristics Steven so liked in another man: blond hair, blue eyes, compact physique, firm ass, and mildly hirsute. And…oh, yes…butch. Out of all the names and information David had fed the computer, Beynor had been the first recommendation of the electronic brain when it had been asked to select the one hustler best suited, among those submitted, for a successful seduction of Steven Gladson. After having just personally testing Beynor in bed, David was assured the computer was right.

He stretched languidly on the bed and daydreamed about how it would be if he could finagle backing from the Gladson Entertainment conglomerate for his latest talent discovery.

The bathroom door opened and Beynor came back into the room.

"You'll do nicely," David said, half to himself, half to Beynor. "You'll do very nicely, indeed."

Beynor didn't reply. He see-sawed the thick Turkish towel between his legs, enjoying the roughness of its cloth as it sucked up the remaining moisture from his shower. He didn't know yet whether or not he should be pleased with David's statement or not. David hadn't gone into any specifics about what he now had planned. So far, for the money he'd been paid, Beynor couldn't complain. After all, David wasn't the type who usually paid for sex. With his good body and good looks, and affiliation with the music business, David, more often than not, likely got "it" free. Beynor had seen a gamut of less attractive—although decidedly younger—men than David actually make a living on the hustling circuit.

"Get dressed, and I'll take you for drinks," David said. Since he was convinced Beynor was satisfactory, they might as well begin plotting that very evening. Steven Gladson would, perhaps, be somewhere downtown if he wasn't overseeing a recording session. Of course, David could call Gladson Entertainment and try to ferret out of Steven's secretary just where Steven would be that evening, but doing that didn't always work, especially these days, what with Steven continually accosted by managers and agents with news of some potentially hot, new, young, and talented rock star on the horizon. With twelve top artists under his wing, Steven didn't need any more in his company's lineup, nor was he looking. Besides which, David was no longer the powerhouse agent in the industry he'd once been.

Beynor continued drying while David took his turn in the bathroom. When David returned, he took up a position in one of the chairs, facing Beynor who was dressed and sitting on the bed.

"Where do we go from here, besides for drinks?" Beynor asked.

"I want you to go to bed with somebody for me," David said, deciding that it would be ridiculous to be anything but candid.

Here it comes, Beynor thought. It wasn't that the situation was new for him. It usually just meant that the "other" person referenced was usually far from being a prime specimen.

"He's neither old nor decrepit, if that's what you're thinking," David said with a laugh, having read Beynor's expression exactly as it occurred.

Beynor didn't reply. He'd heard that line before. It usually meant the guy in question was as *real* loser. He waited, though, for David to continue.

One of the reasons Beynor had made it so big in his particular line of work was that he had long ago realized that he was capable of doing "it" with anyone or anything. It was quite easy for him to imagine even the ugliest old man as some handsome young stud. Besides, it was always logical to assume the price paid him for bedding some fossil, especially one for whom David was pimping, would be substantial. If that were the case, Beynor knew he'd be physically "up" for the occasion, no matter what.

David surveyed Beynor quickly, wondering if he should go ahead and spill the whole plot. It would be a lot easier to get what he wanted if Beynor were completely on board. However, David knew he wasn't dealing with just any ordinary hustler off the streets. Beynor would be quick to realize who and what Steven Gladson was. It wouldn't be smart to have Beynor foul up David's plans by formulating any of his own.

"When do I bed him?" Beynor asked.

"It may take some time getting that moment lined up," David said. "At the moment, this other individual doesn't even know yet he's going to get lucky."

The expression on Beynor's face didn't change.

"Will you want me available at specific times of the day and night?" Beynor asked. His tone was purely business. David wondered how many times this cool young man had discussed his body as if it were just one more piece of merchandise on the open market.

"I'll want you available on call, day or night, until it's done," David said. "You'll be more than adequately compensated for your time and effort. As a matter of fact, if you succeed with this, there'll be a sizable bonus for you."

"Very well," Beynor said.

David thought Beynor might squabble about price and was glad he didn't. Any idiot would have known David talked substantial cash without needing to pinpoint the exact amount. David was glad he hadn't underestimated Beynor's intelligence. David had a tendency to be generous for favors, and it would have been ridiculous for Beynor to haggle.

"Is this going to entail a seduction, or will you just deliver the goods up on a silver platter?" Beynor asked.

"I'm not sure," David admitted. "We'll have to play it by ear."

Since Beynor had already dressed, David got up from his chair and began to put on his own clothes.

"This other party is a friend of yours." Beynor hadn't made it a question.

"No," David admitted.

"Then, I hope you're prepared for the eventuality that he doesn't find me in the least attractive," Beynor warned.

"He'll find you attractive all right," Beynor assured.

"You're sure about that?" Beynor asked. "Different people have different tastes, especially as to what they enjoy in the bedroom."

"I've researched you and my subject well," David said, realizing the more Beynor knew the better the chances for hooking Steven and reeling him in. However, the more Beynor knew, the more dangerous it could be to David's plans, if, say, Beynor, himself, was an amateur singer with aspirations for stardom. In which case, the hustler, as an aspiring artist, might well use his time with Steven to promote himself, rather than David's client. Or, maybe, Beynor would decide Steven could offer him more money for sex than David was paying. "I programmed the needs of the man in question into a computer, and your name popped out the other end."

"That seems an awfully lot of bother to provide sex to someone who doesn't know you're doing him the favor."

"I'm counting on you to make my largesse known to him—eventually."

"Who is this special someone, then?" Beynor asked.

David took a deep breath. "Steven Gladson."

"Doesn't ring a bell," Beynor said. "From the look on your face, I would presume that it should?"

David was, indeed, taken back...just a bit. He'd assumed Steven was known by *everyone,* forgetting that the music industry, as it stood, was a world all its own. Just because Steven, at twenty-four, had become a millionaire, didn't mean everyone not affiliated with the music business knew the how and why. David rechecked his companion and concluded Beynor's ignorance was genuine.

"He owns a recording label among other things," David said. "Actually, he has a lot of the big-name recording artists under contract."

"Oh," Beynor replied.

"*The Funky Turtle*," David ventured the name of one such group with current majority popularity. Their concept album had topped *Billboard* charts for the past three consecutive weeks."

Curiously, Beynor, without a clue, waited for some additional information.

"It's a very popular music group," David said, now dressed except for his shoes. He sat back in the chair.

"Oh," Beynor said again.

David was about to launch into a genuinely detailed explanation of his plan—now that he was quite sure Beynor could pull it off without including some secret personal agenda—but his attention was diverted by the wind-chime sounding of his doorbell. His look indicated that no one was expected. Nonetheless, he went to see who it was.

"My God, what are *you* doing here?" David was surprised to see Travis Butcher who was the whole reason David was conspiring to have Steven Gladson seduced.

"Sally got a check from her dad," Travis said, motioning over his shoulder toward the car parked at the curb. "She thought I looked hungry. I stopped by to borrow a few bucks, since I don't want her to think I'm completely tapped out."

David ushered Travis into the living room, watching for the young man's reaction to Beynor's presence.

Travis was well aware of his manager's homosexual preferences, obviously disapproving without coming right on out and saying so... probably because of whom David was and what he could do for Travis if he set his mind to it. While David found Travis's puritanical attitude more than a little annoying, it wasn't enough to turn him off to the kid's talent.

No denying that Travis was one handsome hunk who, with a bit more meat on his bones, to go with his weighty talent, could, if given the right chance, likely knock the world on its ass, music fans, girls *and* boys, falling into love-struck swoons at his feet. It had been the "and boys" part that had initially gotten David really excited about Travis's potential. Granted, the singer wasn't exactly hung like a horse, but there were ways of making even more substantial inadequacies look impressive in the tight-fitting costumes worn by performers on stage.

"Travis, this is Beynor. Beynor, Travis. Travis has stopped by to pick up some back salary he's owed."

"David's a good agent," Travis told Beynor, obviously misconstruing the relationship between the other two men in the room. "If anyone can make you a success in the music business, he can."

Realizing Travis assumed Beynor a fellow entertainer, David left it at that; with, thank God, no denials from Beynor. David pulled out his wallet and counted off a few bills. Had Travis suspected Beynor was a hustler, he likely wouldn't have been nearly so at ease. He was always made paranoid by his ongoing assumption, probably right, at least most of the time, that most homosexuals who met him were hot to get him out of his clothes and into bed. If a lot of people merely *imagined* they were continually sized up by queers, it wasn't all imagination in Travis's case.

Then, Beynor potentially ruined the mood by saying, "I'm sure if I were a performer, I'd be knocking on David's door."

"You're not in the music business, then?" Travis asked.

David held his breath. He could tell from Travis's continuing easy manner that it still hadn't registered what Beynor and David had been doing before Travis arrived.

"I'm afraid not. I'll have to leave that to the more talented people, like you."

Travis blushed. Oh, yes, he could still blush. That was part of his charm—all that seeming naïveté packaged in otherwise stereotypically masculine sensuality.

"Has David at least played you one of my demos?" Travis asked.

Which led David, with a silent sigh of relief, to conclude Travis's blush was from the pleasure of having been called "talented" by Beynor, rather than from suddenly seeing Beynor as a queer on the make.

Hopefully, Beynor wouldn't let the cat any farther out of the bag. Certainly, he was too much of a professional to indicate any immediate interest in Travis, especially on a sexual level, what with a paying client in the room. When a high-paid callboy was already with someone, it just wasn't proper business etiquette for him to go shopping around for another.

"Travis refers to a demonstration CD," David clarified for Beynor's benefit, simultaneously handing Travis the requested folded bills.

"Oh," Beynor said. "I'm afraid I haven't heard one, but I'll certainly hold out hopes, since David speaks so highly of your work."

"David is great," Travis said and smiled. His face had come alive with Beynor's latest compliment, and David knew the kid didn't get that way because of every compliment fed him during the course of each and every day. So, what was there about Beynor's words that had made them any different?

"…next Wednesday."

Again, David came out of his thoughts, realizing that, this time, he'd missed part of the conversation altogether. By the expressions of Travis and Beynor, David suspected he was apparently expected to respond.

"That is all right, isn't it?" Travis asked. "I mean, we always have people around the studio."

Next Wednesday? David remembered that Travis was cutting another demonstration disc that day. It was a song Travis had written. He was a good song writer. In fact, if he could ever be persuaded to write a love song, it would probably garner all sorts of favorable talk within the music industry. So far, none of his lyrics even touched on love, not even the heart-break of it; which was stranger than hell in an industry where that particular subject was pretty much every song writer's bread and butter.

"I really would like to come," Beynor said.

"Why not?" David conceded with a shrug. He had no doubts but that Travis would never have extended the invitation, though, had he known just what Beynor did for a living. To have refused the request, at this time, however, would have been cause for some sort explanation as to the why-not.

"Good," Travis said and smiled. "It's settled, then."

David thought he detected something, and, then, thought he had to have imagined it. How stupid was he to believe his young singer suddenly was genuinely interested in this blond-haired hustler?

"David will get you a pass," Travis said, and a dimple suddenly appeared in his right cheek that David, surprisingly, didn't ever recall seeing there before.

"Great," Beynor decided.

Travis, though, still didn't make any move to leave. David thought of Sally Coral waiting in the car. Sally was nineteen and had fucked every rocker, or potential rock star, she could get her hands on. She had a father, with deep pockets, somewhere back east who paid her expenses. She would take her temporary lovers to dinner in payment for their stud services. It was often far more soothing to a performer's ego to accept food for sex than actual money. Artists were funny that way, and Sally had a knack for capitalizing on just that idiosyncrasy.

"Would you and Sally like to join us for a drink?" David asked, merely by way of reminding Travis that he had left the young woman in the car.

"Oh, no," Travis said. "Sally has a little party planned for just the two of us."

David could sense signs in the singer's voice and body language that insinuated he would, actually, have loved leaving Sally to join David and Beynor. Why? It certainly wasn't because of David. David held no illusions about that. Had Travis been interested in David, he would have given voice, or action, to it, some way, well before now. What the hell was it about Beynor, unless David just imagined it, which could hold Travis in the room when a good meal and a sexy broad were waiting?

"Maybe we can all get together some other time," Beynor suggested.

Smart cookie, David thought, thanking God that Beynor had taken charge. If David's suspicions about Travis's reluctance to leave seemed initially unfounded, they received credence upon seeing the expression of disappointment suddenly on the young man's face when the singer realized he'd been dismissed. It was apparent, at least to David, that even another small insistence, by David, or by Beynor, would see Travis and Sally joining them for drinks. Well, Beynor had given David his out, and David was prepared to take advantage.

"Do tell Sally hello," he said and smiled.

Reluctantly, Travis put out his hand to take Beynor's in a firm handshake, and said, "See you Wednesday, then." David and Beynor walked him to the door.

Sally was waiting impatiently in the car.

"My manager," Travis said, settling down beside her.

"I know who the hell David Stoff is," Sally replied. She'd been fucking David's artists long before Travis turned up on the scene. "And who's the other Mr. Studly in the doorway with him."

"Beynor-somebody. I can't remember his last name."

"You-all made quite a threesome," Sally said.

Travis frowned. He knew what she was possibly, possibly not, insinuating, and he didn't like it. For two cents, he would have gotten out and left the jealous bitch sitting by her lonesome. He wouldn't, though, because he was hungry. The meal she would buy would hold him over for quite awhile, especially if he got to take home a doggie-bag. Someday, he might be able to afford eating any time, anywhere, anything, and any place he wanted, but that time wasn't quite yet.

"Are we finally ready to go?" she asked.

She made mundane small talk on their way to the restaurant. Travis watched her, vaguely repulsed by the dampness forming on her forehead and within the sweaty crease of her exposed cleavage.

She continued to chatter, and he lost complete interest. He was painfully aware that he had a hard-on, and that Sally wasn't its cause. That admission reluctantly made, he would make sure it was all hers, once he got the bitch into bed…if he didn't decide just to beat the shit out of her instead.

CHAPTER TWO

From watching all of those *Dr.-This* and *Dr.-That* television self-help programs, Sally Coral knew that children raised in homes with one or more abusive parent were prone, when grown up, to turn abusive themselves. She knew from the horse's mouth that Travis Butcher had an abusive father, confessed to her by Travis, included in his apology for the very first time he'd hauled off and hit her, sending her flying across the room against the wall and giving her a black eye and a bruised back. He was so sorry. He didn't mean it. He'd make it up to her. He blamed his father who used to beat him and his mother. Something tainted in his genes, which he tried his best to control, which he, for the most part, had learned to control. Had he hit her before! No, because, most of the time, he could counteract those inherited impulses. He didn't know why this time had been the exception. He felt miserable. He'd make it up to her somehow. She had to forgive him. Didn't he prove how much he loved her in bed? He couldn't be all bad if the two of them were able to make such sweet sex together.

What she didn't know and couldn't explain, much to her chagrin, was why she put up with it. Never, in her wildest imagination, could she have ever dreamed that she would allow herself to become some idiot man's punching bag. Hitting her once was incomprehensible and unforgivable. Hitting her more than once was, without her going to the police, downright disturbing. More disturbing was the possibility that it was the very fact that the two of them *did* make such sweet sex together that had something to do with her giving him one chance after another after another. She didn't even like to contemplate the reality behind how that sweet sex they made was sometimes all the sweeter if it occurred after a beating or during one; admitting to that would have necessitated admitting something about herself that was just too unfathomable to accept *and* maintain her sanity.

She had to dump Travis, just as she'd dumped all of non-beaters. She was her own woman, in charge of her own destiny. Hell, even her father was resigned by now to her being in control of her own life, he merely sending her monthly checks until her trust fund kicked in when she was twenty-one.

She tried to get comfortable where she sat on the hospital examination table, but she couldn't. She hurt all over and suspected she'd be more comfortable in the chair by the door that had a back on it. She wished the damned doctor would get back. How fucking long did it take him to get her a prescription for pain medicine?

When the doctor did get back, she'd tell him it was Travis, in a fit of inexplicable rage, who did this to her. Put the sick psychopath away, or at least allow her to get a restraining order to protect her from him. She didn't need him. God only knew that there were plenty of other male singers in the music business, many of whom she'd fucked before, many of them still to fuck, major and minor stars, all with bigger cocks, without clinging on to this damaged sonofabitch. A lot of the newcomers would continue to be more than delighted to screw her, without any accompanying beatings, just to enjoy her company and a meal they didn't have to pay for. So what that David Stoff thought Travis was the next up-and-coming major rock star? So what that Travis was handsome as hell, had a body to die for, could fuck like no one she'd ever had fuck her before? How many times had she climaxed that time he'd rode her so long and so hard and so fast in that toilet stall of the CMA Awards? She still wasn't sure, having lost count, because she was barely clinging to consciousness after five.

She turned to the doctor when, after knocking briefly, he came in.

"For the pain," he said, handing her the piece of script. "Don't overdue, because they're addictive."

Could a man, in general, Travis Butcher, in specific, become addictive to the point where a woman could actually ignore the harm he caused just because of the intermittent good times he provided?

"I do have to tell you," the doctor said, "that I'm required by law to report any case of physical abuse."

"Which has what to do with the price of tea in China," Sally wanted to know, "since I fell down exactly six stairs?"

"I know that's what you said."

"I've no abusive father or mother, both of my parents living back east. I have no abusive husband, I'm single. As for my boyfriend, he wouldn't hurt a fly." In fact, she'd once seen Travis actually capture one in a newspaper and turn it loose outside, rather than smash it with a swatter as Sally would have done. What was the irony, if any, to be taken from that?

What could be said of doctors and hospitals who didn't share information, anyway? All this one had to do was check with the hospital across town to find out that Sally had fallen down another flight of stairs, or the same ones, just the month before.

"If you're not feeling better in a week, you should really come back for a check-up."

Sally should have been an actress if she could so easily convince doctors that she'd been abused by an inanimate object rather than by Travis's hands doubled into fists. She'd contemplated majoring in theater, once, but had discarded it as way too much work, fraught with too many chances of rejection. It was so much easier to just proceed as she was, living on the money her family provided, later to tap her own resources (thank-you Granddad!) and enjoy life without all of the bother of any nine-to-five work environment. Not that getting the shit kicked out of her was all that enjoyable, but she was determined, whether she had Travis arrested or not, that she would soon see him out of her life, replaced by someone far more appreciative; no matter that his replacement probably couldn't fuck her anywhere nearly as good as Travis did.

Speaking of Travis, he awaited her in the waiting room, looking all downtrodden and repentant. She'd seen him look that way before, and she'd heard the exact same mantra he was suddenly repeating.

"How are you feeling, baby? Better? Did the doctor give you the okay? Hopefully, at least, that's a prescription for pain pills which we'll get at the drug store on the way home, and, then, see that you're tucked in for a good night's rest. Goddamn, you know how sorry I am that this happened, don't you? But, I'm going to take care of you, nurse you through this, and make it all better. You'll see. Really you will..."

He should have been the actor. If Sally didn't know far better, she might actually believe all of his bullshit.

CHAPTER THREE

Steven Gladson and the kid, Harold Dimns, who Wilton Wedge had picked up for him, off some street, brought their drinks into the bedroom. The two sat down on the edge of the king-size mattress, toasting each other silently before downing the remaining fingers of liquor. Then, they placed their empty glasses side-by-side on the bedside table.

Harold took off his shirt, watching Steven Gladson do the same. He'd been told that he wouldn't find it hard to have sex with Steven, and, now, checking out the man's body, he suspected that wasn't a lie. He eyed Steven's well-put-together physique with a good deal of admiration. Being paid to service someone like this would be a pleasure. Harold would have been tempted to bed this guy for free. Of course, he wasn't about to tell Steven that. You could tell just by looking at the penthouse they were in that the man had plenty of money to spare.

"I want you naked when I am," Steven said. He was anxious to get this over and done. Oh, the kid was okay, but for some reason, Steven just couldn't get all that intensely interested. It wasn't just Harold—Harold? Was that this kid's name? Lately, it was sex in general with which Steven was possibly bored. Or if it wasn't the actual sex, itself, that bored him, then it was the process leading up to it. The time had arrived when he was actually contemplating self-abuse as a substitute for the bother of this kind of male-male relationship.

"No sooner said than done," Harold said. He was finished undressing before Steven had dropped his pants. He went over to Steven, let his finger stray Steven's pectorals and across the man's taut belly to the indented navel. He proceeded to play with the silky strands of encircling hair he found there.

Steven wished the men Wilton got for him off the streets would quit trying to be seductive. Couldn't they understand that he would have preferred it if they just stripped down, lay down, and kept their damned mouths shut? Either Steven was going to have to tell Wilton to make it damned clear that all he wanted was sex, or he was going to have to start telling the young men himself.

When they were finished, Wilton appeared, when summoned. He could tell at a glance that Steven was through for the evening.

"Harold, why don't you come with?" Wilton said.

Harold got the idea and was a little taken aback. For the price he was being paid, he had expected to remain quite a while longer.

"Already?"

"I'm afraid so," Steven said, "although, rest assured, you can keep all the money paid for services rendered." He reached for his robe, draping it around his nakedness. "Get dressed, and Wilton will take care of the details."

Steven left the room. Harold was curious as to his dismissal. However, to Wilton, the scene had been just a replay of several others over the past few months.

Steven went into the living room. He sat down on the couch, leaned back into the cushions and shut his eyes.

What in the hell was wrong with him? Somewhere along the line, something had happened, and he didn't know what it was. Or did he? Was it just a simple case of boredom? Steven *was* bored. He was bored with work; he was bored with people; he was bored with sex. To be in such a state of acute boredom, at his age, didn't portend well for the future.

Where had the excitement gone? When he first started out in the music business, sure, it had been work, but it had also been fun. The fact was that he was probably just too successful, no longer needing to devote himself personally to a group to make it a success. He had twelve entertainers and/or bands under the Gladson Entertainment umbrella, all of them successful. It seemed as if there was nothing to do but sit back and let the money flow in. Probably, he should have left one performer, or one group, exclusively to himself instead of diverting everybody off to the specialists he'd hired. Of course, he seldom had complaints as to how his people handled things. They were, after all, the best in their field and the best money could buy. It was just that they were so goddamned efficient at what they did that Steven had ceased to be much of anything except a figurehead inside his own entertainment network. It wasn't that his signature wasn't required on all documents and paperwork; it was just that it was very seldom he found it necessary to change the wording on any document that got as far as his desk. He had a very competent staff. Had he been eighty-four, instead of twenty-four, he would have been far more content with the existing circumstances. But the energy that had propelled him from nobody to a millionaire in six years was still burning, there, in his guts. Only, these days, it had apparently no place to go.

Wilton ushered a dressed Harold out of the bedroom. Steven, his eyes still shut, heard them but didn't acknowledge anyone's existence until Wilton had deposited Harold in the private elevator and shot it toward street level.

"Christ, what a dud!" Steven complained loudly, knowing Wilton and he were now alone.

Wilton didn't answer. This, too, was a typical replay of what usually happened after one of Steven's most-recent sessions. Wilton waited patiently for the storm to abate.

"Out of all the goddamned men in this city, you would think you could find something better for me than that."

Still Wilton didn't answer. He watched as Steven left the couch and went to the bar. Also, he watched as Steven poured two glasses of Scotch.

"Here," Steven said, bringing Wilton one of the glasses. "You may be a rotten pimp, but you do try your damnedest."

"What *is* the problem?" Wilton asked. He had always felt more like a father to Steven than anything else. A washed-out talent agent when Steven had found and rescued him, Wilton now made more money, as Steven's "man", than he had ever managed on his own. Aside from that, Wilton was happy. He liked Steven. He liked being a part of the music business without wondering whether or not he would be washed up tomorrow. He liked to go home at night to his wife and two snot-nosed kids. Steven had given Wilton security. Wilton would never forget that or be unappreciative.

"You tell me what's the matter," Steven countered. "Here I am with everything, and, yet, I feel like I've got a madman inside of me trying to get out."

Wilton eyed Steven. He could appreciate what he saw, even if he wasn't homosexual. In a way, Wilton wished Steven wasn't gay, because he would have made a great catch for one of Wilton's daughters.

"Find something more to do," Wilton suggested.

"Do you think the president of a company like mine spends his days without plenty of things to do?"

Wilton shrugged. He had no answer, then. If he'd ever had one, he would have suggested it a long time ago.

"I'm going out," Steven said, getting to his feet.

"Where shall I say you are, should someone ask?" Wilton asked.

"Just *out,*" Steven said vaguely. He was tired of sitting in his penthouse. He was tired of going to parties, or hosting them. He was tired of freaking out in someone's bedroom on *blue heavens*, *Christmas trees*, *tooies*, or of him freaking out in his own bedroom on *DOM*, *wedding bells*, or *footballs*. He was just plain tired. And it wasn't the kind of tiredness that needed sleep to disperse it.

He went into his bedroom and started to get dressed. He didn't really know where he was going, but, by God, he was going somewhere.

"You'll be back tonight?" Wilton asked when Steven had pushed the button to summon the elevator back to the penthouse.

"I don't know," Steven said.

"You have a recording session tomorrow at eight," Wilton reminded. "*The Funky Turtle* are recording."

"Higgins can run that without me," Steven said. "Higgins is qualified. He has a list of degrees longer than my dick."

The elevator door opened, revealing the carpeted and mirror-lined compartment.

"You *are* Gladson Entertainment," Wilton reminded. "Don't forget that."

"I won't," Steven assured. He was thankful to the older man for trying to make him feel better, but somehow platitudes weren't what Steven needed to cure his present ills.

He ended up at *The Bullring*. He didn't know why. *The Bullring* went back to his days before making it big. He'd picked up an extra dollar or two, here, hustling, during those frequent days, back when he'd needed cash and hadn't been all that choosy about how he got it. It was one of the few bars from Steven's past that was still going strong.

His entrance caused speculation on the part of patrons already there. He was, these days, to them, a new face. He remembered a time when he had been well known to all the regulars, hustlers and customers. Now, the bartender, likewise, eyed him as the stranger Steven was.

"Bourbon," Steven ordered.

"We've only wine or beer."

"Give me something in a phallic bottle, then," Steven said, wondering why he had ordered bourbon, since *The Bullring* had never served liquor. Christ, it had been forever since he'd last been here.

He watched the bartender, a young man typical for this bar: excellent body in torso-hugging T-shirt, tight jeans, and boots. The guy must have been in his late twenties, butch enough to take care of himself in a fight and smoothly efficient in taking care of drinks. He turned his cool blue eyes from Steven and walked to the cooler. Steven watched the movement of muscular ass pressed through worn denim. He could still recall the time such a sight would have excited him. He wondered why it didn't excite him now.

He took his beer with him to a back table that was, like all the others, morphed from old kegs and barrels. The floor was covered with booze-stained sawdust. There were posters on the walls. Most were worn announcements of past bullfights in Mexico and Spain. Some were of men, in leather pants and motorcycle boots, possessing exceptionally rough handsomeness and standing in decidedly cocky posses. One poster showed a currently popular male movie star stripped to the waist. There was a moth-eaten head of a bull hung by a nail on one wall.

There was a loud crack of a ricocheting cue ball. Steven turned his attention to the activity around the nearby pool table. Two studs were playing, one leaning in for a shot.

A few people in the room moved closer to where Steven sat. One leather-clad number, whose naked hairy chest showed through the open zipper of his jacket, seemed about to make a move, but must have decided against it, because he passed close but headed for the toilet located deeper in the shadows. Steven felt the stud's eyes on him, but he pretended that he didn't. It was strange how familiar it all seemed, but, also, how different it was than how he remembered it.

He took a sip of his beer. The cool lip of the bottle kissed his mouth. He tasted the cold flush of bitter liquid. It had been awhile since he'd enjoyed the simplicity of a good beer. His palate, these days, was much more into liquor, like bourbon. He took another swallow, still not replacing the bottle on the table. He leaned back in his chair, opening his legs to couch the bottom of the bottle against his crotch. He felt the coolness of the glass seep through the material of his pants to his balls. In the dim lighting of the room, the bottle looked like a fat and swollen erection between his thighs.

He waited. He didn't know for what he waited, or even why he waited. Did he want to trick with one of these hustlers? Or did he just come back here to renew an old acquaintance with an atmosphere he somehow missed?

He was halfway through his beer when he divined why he probably hadn't yet been approached, merely sized up. No one in the room was quite sure in what capacity Steven was there. He was possibly too good-looking to be a buyer. Yet, no hustler, who hoped to score in *The Bullring,* would have ever showed up as dressed like an American business mogul as Steven was.

He smiled to himself. Definitely, he was dressed all wrong for this bar. Had he known, before leaving his penthouse, that he would be sitting here, now, he would have found something more appropriate. Somewhere in the back of one of his closets, he still had the proper accoutrements for this establishment. He had the tapered T-shirt that molded his well-developed chest like a second skin. He had the pair of jeans which had rubbed so often over the familiar parts of his body, including his substantial cock and balls, that the denim was starting to fray. That was what one wore in *The Bullring*, not a $2000 Brioni suit.

He went to the bar for a second beer. The bartender eyed him with the same coolly appraising look as before. Steven now knew there was little chance for any action, and he probably should have left. However, he felt even more at ease now that he realized he had succeeded in inadvertently isolating himself from the more intimate action of the bar. He took his beer back to his commandeered table, and its chair, and sat down.

The hairy-chest man finally came back from the bathroom. He had been back there for so long that Steven somehow suspected that he'd likely released more than his bladder in the piss-smelling darkness.

Steven was almost finished with his second beer when Beynor entered the bar. Steven wasn't the only one who saw him. The movement of heads was audible. Beynor dressed for the part. Half of the people in the bar looked upon him as competition, the other half as potential for hot and heavy sex.

He wore a brown suede vest hung open over his bare and muscular chest. The satiny tanned flesh of his pectorals was covered with its mat of light-blond hair. His navel, showing above the waistband of his hip-hugging leather trousers, was sheathed by curling pubic tendrils. The softness of leather clung to his well-shaped legs, molding his crotch sensuously and concealing very little. He wore dark leather boots. Around his neck, he had a gold chain: not one of those effeminate thin chains but a thicker and more masculine complicated interlacing of twisted metal. His straw-blond hair haloed his face which was strikingly handsome, rather than pretty.

The bartender brought him a requested beer, and the question, "You new in these parts?" The bartender was impressed by what he saw, and he had seen more than his share of hunky males for sale. Like any good bartender, he would have liked a few answers, because it would likely only be minutes before there would be a casual trailing of people to the bar to find out from him just what this new stud was interested in doing.

"Actually, I'm not new at all," Beynor admitted, taking it no farther.

"Funny," the bartender said, "but I haven't seen you around."

"I just don't make here very often," Beynor said. During the short conversation, he had surveyed the room and picked out Steven who stood out like a sore thumb. Even men out to pay for an evening of fun and games rarely came into *The Bullring* looking as if they could afford paying any asking price. There were other places where one hustled a different quality of merchandise and more formal dress was the norm; not here.

"Looking for a little extra spending money?" the bartender asked. It wouldn't hurt to latch onto Beynor from the beginning. If this guy could be directed into a few select beds, he and the bartender could make a financial killing.

"Not tonight," Beynor said. "I'm meeting someone."

"Be sure to come back, later," the bartender suggested. "I doubt you're the type to be exhausted by just one session."

"Sounds like a plan," Beynor said, flashing a knowing smile, even though he had no intentions of coming back any time soon.

He took his beer and headed for Steven's table. He felt the admiring stares on his body more than he actually pinpointed their origins. His attention was solely on Steven, watching the man's eyes as they ranged from pure curiosity to actual shock when Beynor brazenly pulled out the spare chair and joined him at the table.

"Hi," Beynor said and smiled. His teeth were white and looked even whiter in contrast to his pleasantly tanned skin. Steven found himself wondering what color the eyes were that went with Beynor's straw-blond hair; in the gloom it was difficult to tell.

"Do I know you?" Steven asked.

"No, but you're going to," Beynor replied. "You don't mind that I joined you, do you?"

"I'm afraid I was just getting ready to leave," Steven answered, wondering why he lied. Beynor's charms weren't wasted, in that Steven actually enjoyed having the handsome man seated across from him. There was something, here, that Steven found missing in the butch boys who had recently passed through his bedroom. Here was a definite aura of masculinity. Not that Steven's tricks were ever silly little twinks. Wilton knew Steven's tastes well enough not to bring him someone effeminate. However, there was butchness, and, then, there was butchness; often as different as night from day.

Beynor shrugged. It would be a shame, after all these days of waiting, to have this smug bastard slip through his fingers. Beynor was finding it more than a tad tiresome to be on twenty-four-hour call, waiting for one of David's spies to spot Steven out in public. Now that Steven had finally been found, out alone, without even the benefit of a shielding entourage, it would be a shame to have to wait for some other opportunity. Beynor remembered David's assurances that Steven's preferences had been fed into a computer, and it had been Beynor's name regurgitated in first response.

"Join me for another drink," Beynor persisted. "I'll buy." Nonchalantly, he scratched the bulge between his legs, letting his fingers linger to make sure Steven's attention had followed along. Beynor had all intentions of doing what David was paying him to do, and do it successfully.

By now, Beynor was well aware that David was no longer at the top of his game. David had made it big once, awhile back, with an effeminate boys' band. He had made a lot of money, and he had spent it. Somewhere along the way, though, David had lost his knack for picking star acts to the point where, while the Steven Gladsons of the music world continued to get richer and richer, David's cash reserves had petered away; David desperately needed someone to help him capitalize upon the obvious talent of Travis Butcher to bail him out.

Beynor had been to the recording studio a couple of times, now, to watch and hear Travis perform, and, as far as he could tell, Travis was just as good as David advertised. Then, again, what in the hell did Beynor know about the music business?

Probably, he could have left Steven, right then and there, and told David there wasn't a chance in hell of Steven ever listening to one of Travis's demos, and David would probably believe him. Beynor had a way of coming across believable. David would still give him his money, since David wasn't the type to fink out on a deal. Beynor, though, liked to think he wasn't the type to fink out, either. Besides, he actually liked David, and Steven certainly wasn't all that hard to look at.

"Come on," Beynor said, standing. "I've decided we're not going to have that drink after all."

"What do you mean … *you*'ve decided?"

"We're going back to your place," Beynor said, "and my hard cock is going to nail you to your bed while you beg for more and more."

Steven thought for sure the whole bar had heard. He glanced hurriedly around the room, thinking he saw straining ears trying to catch even more of the conversation. Despite certain resentment, he found the situation exciting.

"Says who?" Steven asked finally.

"Says me," Beynor answered.

Steven was now *sure* everyone was listening.

"Come on," Beynor said. "You have a recording session at eight tomorrow morning. I'd hate to have you miss it."

"How thoughtful of you," Steven said facetiously, wondering how in the hell this hustler knew Steven's schedule. Likely, the guy was a singer, or member of some group, looking for a break.

"Come on," Beynor persisted.

"I'm staying," Steven said with loudly and with finality.

"You're sure?" Beynor asked.

"I'm staying," Steven insisted.

The bartender, like everyone else in the room who was listening, found himself wondering just who in the fuck these newcomers were.

"Then, if you'll excuse me," Beynor said. "I have to go."

Steven watched him leave. He swallowed his next mouthful of warming beer with an accompanying grimace. After which, he spontaneously got up. God only knew what he expected when he exited the bar onto the sidewalk. Did he actually expect the guy to be waiting for him? If he did, he was sorely disappointed. There were people, but none of them were Beynor. Christ, but Steven didn't even think to get the stud's name. That wasn't how Steven would have operated a few years back. Back in the day, he wouldn't have been such a goddamned jackass. He hadn't found anyone as interesting as this butch number for a damned long time. And he'd blown it.

He returned to the bar, ordered another beer, and, this time drank it while standing where he was, while the bartender watched. Why had he been so uptight? He'd acted like an indignant schoolgirl trying to protect her virginity. Had he been shocked when the young man had bluntly said they should go to Steven's place for sex? Excited, yes. Shocked? Maybe, shocked because the proposition had come when he hadn't really expected it. He was out of touch. He had been brought street boys by Wilton for too long, now. It had seemed easier that way. Sex had become an inconvenience best gotten out of the way as quickly as possible without the mating dance required in gay bars.

He finished his drink. Then, he asked the bartender if he knew the young man with whom Steven had been conversing. The look he got told him the bartender knew even less than Steven. It had been such a goddamned silly question to ask. He had been the one sitting with the young man. He, more than anyone in the room, should have known his name.

Again, Steven left the bar. Each step, he found himself looking at the faces that passed him. Each proved a disappointment. He kept thinking of the blond hair, the eyes which would have probably proved blue in the light, the compact and muscular body, the impressive contours of the crotch; all of which had been offered up to Steven like some exotic dish at a banquet, and Steven had rejected it.

He hadn't really expected Beynor to leave. He realized that now. It was the surprise of his apparently disinterested shrug, and his departure, after the blatant lead-in, which had thrown Steven really off balance. It had seemed inconceivable that the guy would make so hurried an exit, just because Steven had attempted to assert his dominance over the situation, just as he always tried to dominate any situation. Only this time, he hadn't succeeded. Also, he knew, now, that he had early-on, at least subconsciously, decided to go home with the man the moment Beynor had been seated at the table.

He turned the corner to get to his car. Beynor leaned against the car's fender.

"Decided to change your mind, did you?" Beynor said with a wide grin.

"Confident bastard, aren't you?" Steven said. "How did you know this was my car?"

"How many people drive a car this expensive into this area of town? Besides, there was a paid informer who followed you from your apartment earlier this evening."

"Sounds like a lot of fucking bother," Steven said. Now that he'd found Beynor again, he, also, found the same interplay of emotions that had caused him to lose out before. Why in the hell couldn't he just admit he had come chasing him out of *The Bullring* like one of those bulls chasing a runner in Pamplona? The fucker probably knew it anyway. Beynor looked damned confident, propped against the fender.

"Just what is it you want?" Steven asked finally.

"I thought I made that perfectly clear in the bar," Beynor said.

"And what makes you think that I want the same? And don't tell me a little bird told you."

"I don't need a little bird to tell me when another guy is turned on," Beynor said confidently.

"Bullshit!" Steven determined. So what that he was aroused and had been since Beynor had arrived in the bar?

He unlocked the car door and got in. He leaned to release the lock on the other door, expecting Beynor to get in beside him. The door remained shut.

"Bastard!" Steven mumbled under his breath. He knew what he wanted to do—or, rather *not* what he wanted to do, but what he *should* do. He should drive the car away and leave the fucker standing there without a prayer. As if he might play out the action, he activated the car ignition to engage the engine. Still, Beynor didn't get in. Steven put the car in gear, released the emergency brake and drove forward. Out of the corner of his eye, he saw Beynor still making no move to stop him. Beynor was almost where he had been when Steven had arrived, only having stepped back slightly to let the car slide away beside him.

Steven stopped the car and waited. Beynor didn't make a move. Steven, though, was prepared only to go so far. What did the Mexicans call it? *Machismo.* Yes, it was a question of *machismo,* if he understood the term correctly. Beynor couldn't expect Steven to give overly much. Steven had already made his reciprocal interest more than apparent. Nothing happened. Another Mexican term came to mind: Mexican standoff.

He lowered the window. Finally, Beynor moved.

"Trouble with your car?" Beynor asked, squatting so his head was eye-level with Steven.

"Get in," Steven said. "I'm in a hurry."

"Go ahead and go," Beynor said. "I guarantee you, I won't be found leaning against your front door when you get home."

"And if I drive away, that will be the last you'll ever see of me," Steven promised. "It's a stupid man who won't compromise just a little."

"Right," Beynor said. He stood, moved around the car and opened the passenger-side door. He got in, smiling widely. "I may be many things, but I'd hate to think myself stupid."

Steven drove them into the line of traffic. He'd committed himself, and he wasn't really sure if he'd lost a certain amount of face in doing so.

"It is a stupid man who doesn't realize the advantages of compromise, isn't it?" Beynor said, reading Steven's thoughts.

Neither said anything else for another five minutes.

"You're something of a bastard, do you know that?" Steven said, finally, not looking at Beynor.

"I'll admit I had a certain advantage," Beynor said. "If that makes me a bastard, then I suppose I am."

They drove the freeway, its lights reflecting through the windshield. Finally, Steven chanced a glance in Beynor's direction. The young man sat comfortably in the bucket seat. While Steven looked, Beynor turned to him, in response, and smiled.

"You don't get picked up very often, do you?" Beynor grinned. "Usually, it's the other way around, is it? You should really let it happen this way more often."

"I'll keep that in mind," Steven said facetiously. "In the meantime, what is it that you really want from me?" He sighted the exit that he wanted on the freeway and began weaving through the traffic to get to it. His place wasn't but minutes away. He felt a tightening in his gut. Certainly, Wilton would be surprised. Steven hadn't picked up anyone by himself in quite awhile. It wouldn't take Wilton but a second to look and know this one had to be somehow different.

"Haven't we been through this before?" Beynor answered.

"It's only because of your unsatisfactory answer, the first time around, that I'm asking now," Steven replied.

"You're telling me, in a roundabout way, that you don't consider yourself attractive enough to warrant being propositioned by a stud like me in a gay bar without some hidden agenda?"

"You have such a magnificent command of the English language," Steven said sarcastically.

"Must we discuss motive before we've even gone to bed?" Beynor asked.

"Then, there *is* an ulterior motive?"

"Obviously, you do suspect as much," Beynor reminded. "It's not so much how we found each other, anyway. It's just that we did, don't you agree?"

"If you have anything in mind, besides sex, you should contact my secretary," Steven said with deceptive coolness. He pulled the car onto the circular approach to his building.

"Sure, I should," Beynor agreed with a wide grin, "but I've discovered that it's often the unorthodox methods that get the best results. Besides I've always preferred dealing with the man on top instead of bottom men." What he'd just said was rife with double-entendre.

Steven stopped the car in his parking space. The night-guard hardly looked up as they passed. The elevator, activated by Steven's key card, brought them swiftly and smoothly to the penthouse.

Wilton met them at the top. He had his coat on and a muffler thrown around his neck, although the weather was hardly cool enough to warrant his wearing either.

"I was just leaving," he said. He didn't comment on Beynor. What was there to say, after all? He could tell, at a glance, that Steven had succeeded in picking up more of a man than Wilton had managed lately. Confidentially, he hoped this new one had some luck in entertaining Steven, because Wilton's boss really needed something, or someone, to knock him out of his lethargy.

"I've decided to spend the evening in," Steven said. "Say hello to Helen and the girls."

"Will do," Wilton replied and stepped into the vacated elevator. The door closed, WHOOSH, behind him.

"Now, shall we talk?" Steven asked, going to the bar for a drink. Despite the beer he'd consumed that evening, he needed something far stronger.

"Aw, let's go to bed and fuck you shitless, instead," Beynor countered. "Or, if you really insist, vice-versa."

CHAPTER FOUR

Travis finished his fifth song. He was sweating heavily. Perspiration bathed his face, burning his eyes. Beneath his arms, it was like warm soup. His lips were dry.

"He'll need new material," Steven said.

Travis couldn't see Steven, couldn't see anything because of the sweat in his eyes, and the Klieg lights focused directly on him. Steven and the others were somewhere in the shadows that were the center of the room.

"They're *his* songs, Steven," David said. "The kid wrote them."

"They just don't cut it for what I would have in mind," Steven said. "If I took him on, I'd have Carl Trine do some lyrics, maybe Eric Dwingt on the music. That is, *if* I took him on. Have him sing that one, again, about the beauty of death."

"Travis," David's voice emerged from the darkness. "Give us number three once again, will you?"

Travis adjusted the guitar strap on his shoulder, tuned a couple of strings on his guitar that were on the brink of sounding hinky, and began to play and sing. For a few minutes, he became lost in his own little world, oblivious to everything else. He could easily get lost in his music, which he found even more enjoyable than sex. It was soothing to become so disappeared among the intricate patterns of chords, melodies, notes, and words. As soon as the song was finished, though, he was, like now, always plunged too quickly back into a reality far less comforting.

"He'd need a back-up group," Steven said before Travis's last note had faded.

"God, Steven, isn't he good enough as he is?"

"You want me in on this, and he has to have a back-up group," Steven said; he knew just the one to use, after he'd rename them. "You came to me, because I know my business. Well, I'll tell you that if he's going to make it, it'll be with a group, even if he gets main billing. No one makes shit anymore with just a stool, a guitar, and an otherwise empty stage."

The spotlights went out. Travis blinked to become accustomed to the resulting gloom. Steven and David walked toward him from their chairs. Off to one side, Beynor leaned against one of the plaster pillars that supported the ceiling. Travis was glad Beynor was there.

Steven and David stopped a couple of feet from the singer. Travis slipped off the stool, gently placing his guitar on the spot just vacated. He looked at Steven. It seemed strange that so much depended upon what Steven thought when the young man was only a couple months Travis's senior.

"You want to make it to the big time? Steven asked. It was apparent he was addressing his questions to the singer.

"Who doesn't?" Travis replied.

"Actually, in final analysis, a lot of people don't — really," Steven said. "Does that surprise you? Maybe, it does, but it's true. A lot of people just *think* they want to make it. Those who genuinely know they want it also know that it's not going to be an easy row to hoe. You have to make all sorts of sacrifices along the way. You have to compromise, sometimes even your ideals. It's a stupid man who doesn't know where to compromise, isn't that right, Beynor?"

Beynor had left his place, against the plaster pillar, and was now sitting half-on, half-off, a desk on the periphery of the group. Apparently, he found something amusing about what Steven said, because he answered not verbally but with a wide smile. Travis saw it as some kind of "in" joke, a personal exchange, between Steven and Beynor. Travis didn't think he liked Steven. As a matter of fact, he definitely *didn't* like him, and not just because Steven was gay.

"It's another world up on top," Steven said, still addressing Travis. "Ask David about the top. He was up there once. The air is thin, and you get so lightheaded, at times, that you can easily imagine that you're destined to stay there forever. Then, when you least expect it, you're tumbling down the mountain. Someone else has sneaked to the summit and given you the mighty heave-ho. It's a long pull to the top, buster. It's damned hard to stay put once you make it. And, it's a fucking long, but, sometimes, mighty fast slide from the top back to the very bottom."

"He has what it takes," David assured. "I feel it. You must feel it, too."

"Take off your shirt," Steven said. For a quick instant, Travis didn't know to whom Steven addressed the request. Suddenly, he realized it had been directed at him.

"My shirt?"

"Yes," Steven said. "If you've under there what I think you do, it's a shame to cover it up."

"What's taking off my shirt have to do with my music?"

"Just take it off," Steven said. "Your manager, here, seems to think that I know more about the business than he does, and he's right, both of us having been around a helluva lot longer than you have. So, why don't you just stop asking questions and do what you're asked to do? If you're only asked to take off your shirt to get to the top, that's far less than some others have had to lose on their way up the ladder."

There wasn't a person in the room who missed the connotation. Travis looked uncomfortable.

"Go on, Travis, take it off," David cajoled. The two were so close to reaching the big time that David could taste it. If it didn't happen, now, he knew that it would likely never happen. That was a frightening realization. Sometimes, he woke up in a cold sweat in the middle of the night, having dreamed he was hanging over a chasm, having used up his last inch of rope. If Steven didn't throw the lifeline, here and now, there was no longer much hope of David going anywhere but farther down.

Finally, Travis complied, assuaged by Steven's tone having remained entirely business-like throughout. There'd been no sexual implications or undertones. Travis knew if there had been, he would have spotted them. Awkwardly, he held tightly to his removed piece of clothing.

"Imagine all the panting fairies and teenie-bopper little girls when we show that to them on stage," Steven said. If he hadn't been so personally involved, at the moment, with Beynor, he might have found Travis attractive in more than a purely business way. As it was, Steven was merely concentrated on the business-potential of the piece of merchandise he was being offered. The young man exuded masculinity, tempered with a certain naïveté that would have queers and straights, boys and girls, alike, drooling in the aisles and in the mosh pits. Travis was the first property Steven had seen in a long time that he felt from the get-go could be targeted toward a very wide audience, indeed. Other artists had claimed bisexuality, but few of them really pulled it off. Here was someone who, whether he was or not, at least *looked* the part.

"Perform without my shirt?" Travis thought he'd misunderstood.

"My God, it's a perfect idea!" David said.

"If you're a real performer, you can perform buck naked," Steven said.

"I'm a singer, not a stripper," Travis insisted.

"There are a lot of good singers around," Steven said. "I see some of them every goddamned day of the week. But, in this day and age, being good at singing isn't always enough. I'm not too sure it's ever been. You have to have a gimmick. You've always had to have one, really. I'm telling you that if you strip down to the waist, wear a pair of tight faded blue jeans with the top button undone, you have a chance…just a chance…of making the big time. The whole thing boils down to just how badly you want the golden ring on the merry-go-round. You think it over, and let me know. You *and David* think it over. But don't either of you take too damned long. It's only with some misgiving that I'm even considering handling you. My company already has a full roster. Get too many over the limit, and I'll start hearing belly-aching about how I'm not giving all of my artists the attention they think they deserve."

Beynor gave Travis a wide smile before following Steven out of the room. Travis watched Beynor go, somehow disappointed that he'd left. For some reason, strange, Travis would have liked a few drinks with Beynor, just a bit of man-to-man bonding that could never happen between Travis and David. David was okay, but all he thought about was getting back on the top of the music-business pyramid. David would have agreed with Steven if the latter had insisted Travis strip completely naked and prance around on stage with a blatant hard-on.

"You're in!" David literally squealed when Beynor and Steven had let the studio door swing shut between them. "Jesus, we're *both* in."

"I'm not going to do it, David," Travis said, putting his shirt back on.

"You're not going to do what?" David asked. He couldn't believe his ears. It was like finding the lifeline for which he'd been waiting for a seeming eternity, only to have it sliced just as he was grabbing hold.

"I'm not taking of any of my clothes so that thousands of screaming fairies can ogle."

"It's a gimmick," David said. "Every performer has to have a gimmick."

"I don't need a gimmick," Travis said. "I'm a good singer."

"Don't be a fool as well! Of course, you can sing. Steven wouldn't touch you if you couldn't."

"Steven is a homosexual!"

"And so am I," David reminded. "Since when did you let that stop you from using me as a manager?"

Travis didn't answer. What in the hell could he answer? Nothing. David *was* a homosexual. Travis had always *known* it, and David had never made any bones (boners?) about it. Travis hated homosexuals, and, yet, he, invariably found himself drawn to them, and vice-versa, until he was surrounded by them. Why? What was there about him that sent out false signals like a moth in heat to attract every horny same-sex moth from miles around? He only wished he knew. If he could pinpoint the fault, he would have gladly cut it out.

"Listen to me very carefully, Travis," David said. "I know how you feel about gays. But you're too good-looking not to be seen attractive by members of your own sex. Goddamnit! Whether you like it or not, you've certain availability stamped all over you, and it's time you started taking advantage of it, instead of pretending it doesn't exist."

Travis hit him. Not expecting the blow, David took it full on the jaw. The punch literally lifted him off the floor. He fell back into the desk and, then, over it. It was a weird sensation. It was almost like standing apart and watching the whole thing happening to someone else.

"I'm *not* a faggot!" Travis's voice came from a seemingly very long ways away. Then, David felt a pain in his side, realizing from within a kind of stupor that Travis had just kicked him. There was more pain and a sudden remembrance of Sally Coral who had recently been released from the hospital after she'd been admitted with a bruised face and two broken ribs. She had insisted she had fallen down the stairs. David passed out.

The blackness finally faded to gray, the gray to an opaque haze that came complete with a dark blob that swam through it. Accompanying all of this was an unmistakable feeling of dampness and a buzzing which took every bit of a minute to be distinguished as someone's voice.

"Are you all right?"

David recognized the voice before the face completely focused.

"Beynor?"

"What in the hell happened?"

"Nothing."

"Nothing?" Beynor helped David to his feet and, then, to a nearby chair. "I'd certainly hate to see what you'd look like if something *had* happened."

"It was just a little accident," David said.

"Looks like you and Sally Coral fell down the same flight of stairs," Beynor said.

David laughed as best he could, but quickly stopped, because of a sudden ache in his jaw.

"Don't tell Steven about this, will you?" David asked. Now that his head was clearer, he glanced hurriedly around the room to make sure that Steven hadn't returned with Beynor.

"*The Funky Turtle* are having a recording session down the hall," Beynor said, sensing David's thoughts. "Steven missed the last one and thought he'd better catch this one. I came back to join Travis and you in celebration, but it looks as if you two decided to have it without me. Some blast it must have been, by the looks of you when I came in."

"We all have our little problems," David said.

"Do we all beat up women and agents?" Beynor asked. There was certain levity in his question that David didn't miss; David grinned, noticed new pain throughout his face.

"I would prefer that he'd stuck to resilient women," David said. "This old homosexual isn't used to getting thrown around a room."

"What *did* happen?" Beynor asked.

"Travis *should* be gay," David said, deciding that Beynor must already know that piece of obvious information. Surely, Beynor had been around long enough to know that Travis's interest in him was more than fraternal, even if Travis refused to admit it even to himself. "I know that's a stock phrase we all use for straights we'd like to screw, or would like to have screw us, but with Travis it really does apply. He has sexual drives he refuses to admit. What do you do with a person like that?"

"May I suggest staying as far away from him as possible?"

"You do have a sense of humor," David said. "I like that."

"Come on," Beynor said. "I'll take you home."

"I have to talk to Travis first."

"Travis can wait until tomorrow," Beynor said. "Let him cool down for awhile. Steven doesn't expect either of you to give him an answer this very evening."

"I handled it wrong with Travis," David said. "I was so anxious that he was going to gum up this opportunity that I lost my cool."

"Travis will come around," Beynor said. "He just needs a little time to put his rationalizing mechanism into higher gear."

"He doesn't think I'm handling his career with his well-being in mind," David said. "He doesn't really think I care about him as a person. He thinks I'm only interested in him, because I need someone, anyone, to get me back on top. And do you know what? I sometimes wonder if he's not right. It's grand up there on the top of the mountain. Once you've been there, it's harder than hell to deal with existing anywhere else."

"You'll get there again," Beynor assured. "You just might want to be careful who you bring along with you."

David looked into Beynor's eyes. Beynor was kneeling beside the chair, still holding the damp rag he'd been using to sponge David's forehead when David regained consciousness.

"You probably find this all very silly, don't you?" David divined.

"Not any sillier than people in any other business," Beynor said.

"Music just isn't *any other* business," David said. "I know it's hard for you to see that, having been dropped into this, suddenly, from the outside. But music *is* something else. It's part of my body, my blood, my mind, even if it is full of prima donnas and people who can't adjust to success or to the lack of it. I wouldn't ever want to be doing anything else."

Beynor stood and tossed the wet rag onto the top of the nearby desk. The wind that resulted from the loud *plop* elevated desk-top papers.

"You'll need to go home for a nice rest," Beynor said.

David wrapped his arms around Beynor's muscular legs, his cheek pressing tightly into the young man's crotch. He held tightly for a moment without saying anything. When he finally did, it was in a low whisper.

"It's so lonely sometimes. I wake up some nights and just wish that there was someone there with me. Someone I could just hold for a minute. Not just for the sex, don't you see? Something more. I need someone to tell me that everything will be all right, that I just had another nightmare, and all will go away. I think Travis must feel that way sometimes, and so I try to understand. But, Christ it's hard."

David wasn't feeling sorry only for himself. He was sorry for all those who never allowed themselves to let go: like Beynor who would probably never understand, because he had emptied his life of emotions he'd long ago come to consider a hindrance in the business of selling himself for sex; like Travis who had trapped all of his emotions inside of him and refused to let them come out.

"I'll bet you meet a lot of kooks, like me, in your line of business," David said.

"Come on, David, let's get your ass in gear, and I'll give you a ride home."

"You go," David said, giving Beynor's legs a quick squeeze. "Steven probably is wondering where you disappeared to."

"It will likely do Steven a world of good to be kept waiting for a couple more hours."

"You do like him, don't you?"

Beynor hesitated, knowing any answer was likely to be misinterpreted. Knowing David, Beynor sensed the man was insinuating far more into the definition of "like" than Beynor ever would or could.

"I wouldn't read anything more into our relationship than it is…a business arrangement."

"I would have hoped for a bit more," David said. "From what I've seen, you're the first person Steven has kept around, steady, in over two years."

"You're a helpless romantic," Beynor chided.

"And you're too much the opposite," David said. He got to his feet, finding that he was far weaker than he thought. Momentarily, he took hold of the chair's back for support. He saw that Beynor hadn't missed any of it.

"You're sure you're all right?" Beynor asked.

"Fine," David affirmed. "You go ahead and find Steven. Keep telling him what a piece of hot property he's going to get with Travis."

"You do plan on delivering Travis, then?"

"He'll come around," David assured.

Beynor went to the door, giving a small wave as he passed through it and into the hallway beyond. It was only a short distance to the studio *The Funky Turtle* was using. A security guard passed Beynor through with just a brief nod. Beynor had become a well-recognized face around the studio complex as of late. It was rumored, by more than just Steven's acquaintances, that the young record mogul had officially taken Beynor as his other half. At first, Beynor hadn't known if he liked the talk or not. Finally, he indulged it, because he figured it wouldn't be bad publicity, considering his profession. He was meeting more than a few people with money who could be good contacts after Steven and he were through. That Steven and his relationship was due, eventually, to undergo a cooling—despite the present heat—was something he accepted as fact. No relationship lasted forever. One merely had to utilize whatever the few precious moments of its existence to glean whatever value one could milk from it.

Steven beckoned to him from the other side of the room. The technicians were preparing for a playback. *The Funky Turtle*, six in all, were lounging about with paper cups of coffee. Steven looked as if he was bored with the whole affair (frankly, he was), and was anxious for Beynor's company.

"Well?" Steven queried.

"Our singer really gave poor David a beating."

"You suspected as much." It wasn't a question. There was a quick blurt of music and voices from the loudspeakers. It aborted after just a few seconds. More adjustments were made, utilizing electronic dials and knobs behind the glass shielding that separated performers from the machinery that would eventually have their music perfected and preserved for the screaming masses.

"Travis has done it before," Beynor said.

"You mean little Sally Coral?" Steven said. "Everyone knows."

"Makes Travis a bit tainted, doesn't it?"

"Travis idolizes you, Beynor. Maybe, it's even something more. Surely, you've seen the way he looks at you."

"If Travis heard you say that, you'd probably be the next body on the recording-room floor."

Steven laughed, stopped only by the announcement that the latest playback was ready. He gave the signal for the go-ahead, and everyone settled down to listen. When the recording was finished, Steven didn't seem too happy with what he'd heard. He stood up and went to a man dressed in a business suit who was apparently the executive in charge of the session. After a few minutes of muted discussion, Steven turned to leave the room. He motioned for Beynor to follow.

"The group is getting sloppy," Steven said when Beynor and he were in the hallway. "People have a tendency to do that once they've too long breathed the rarefied air at the top. They're fools, though, to think their sloppiness won't lubricate their eventual fall. Sloppy fools like them make way for people like your young Travis."

"He's hardly *my* Travis."

"Isn't he?"

"David doubts he even knows what I really do for a living."

"Then, you and David are both highly underestimating Travis's intelligence," Stevens said. "The music world is just too small for him *not* to know."

"He doesn't like homosexuals."

"That's probably why he *pretends* he doesn't know you're one," Steven ventured.

"Let's talk about something else, shall we?" Beynor suggested.

"Why so loathe discussing the music world's next star?"

"You really think he'll be that, then?"

"I wouldn't take him on if I thought otherwise," Steven said.

"We are assuming, of course, that David can persuade him to team up with you — yet another gay."

"You have any doubts?"

"No," Beynor answered after only a short pause.

"Neither do I," Steven said with a smile. "Travis will go off on his pout for a few hours, and, then, he'll rationalize the taking off of his shirt in public and the stuffing of his pants' crotch with a pouch of buckshot to make him look more substantially well-hung. Such small sacrifices, after all, to make for fame and fortune."

They left the building, walking around it to Steven's car.

"Are we going anywhere special?" Beynor asked.

"I thought we'd go back to my place."

"In the middle of the afternoon?"

"They can handle things here," Steven said. When the car door was open, he got in. Beynor climbed in beside him. "They've been handling things very well for the past few years. As soon as I take personal charge of Travis's career, I'll have very few minutes for relaxation; so, I want to enjoy some fun while I can. You didn't have anything else planned, did you?"

"Do you know, since I've begun running around with this particular crowd, I've had very little time for my regulars. When I get back on call, I'm going to have to build a whole new clientele."

"You play your cards right, Beynor, and when you're done with this little crowd, you won't have to worry about going back into hustling."

Beynor leaned back in the seat, shutting his eyes to the sun that poured through the window. He didn't press for an explanation. There was no need. It would have taken a fool not to realize that there was money to be made it riding the coattails of any rising star. Of course, he couldn't hope to come away with as much as Steven, David, or Travis. But when one was talking millions of dollars, what in the hell did it really matter whether it was one or twenty-one?

CHAPTER FIVE

Beynor turned up the volume of the television. The host on the late-night show in progress had just introduced *Butcher and the Meat*.

The screen faded for just a second. When the picture came back, it showed Travis and the back-up musicians Steven had selected for him. The camera zoomed in for a close-up of Travis while the group played the short overture to the song he was about to sing.

"He looks even better on TV," Beynor said.

"Yes," Steven agreed. His mind raced to determine which camera angles were the young man's best, what would have to be changed during all following performances. For one, make-up had used too much eye-liner and mascara. Steven wanted Travis's appeal to be to men as well as women, but that didn't necessitate "dragging" his handsome face to make it effeminate. Travis's image was to be butch all the way. When the camera panned back to take in the whole group, Steven's viewpoint was still that of a technician; although, he wasn't so much interested in how good Travis now looked, now, as he was in how the young man might look better in the future.

Travis began to sing. He didn't yet have the stage presence of a total professional, but there was an indication that he would soon learn. His delivery was good. The song was a good vehicle to introduce him to the late-night television audience. It wasn't the song Steven would have preferred, but the show's producers had objected to the original choice, because of language. The show was still considered "for family" despite its time slot.

"He looks very good," Steven admitted finally.

Beynor watched the ripples of Travis's muscles, saw sweat flushing to sheen the bared flesh of the singer's chest and belly. The top button of the faded jeans, undone as Steven had insisted, allowed just a peek at the fan of Travis's pubic hair.

"See how easily he works his audience?" Steven said with a smile, evidently pleased. After Travis's initial outburst and beating of David, the singer, as Steven had predicted, had emerged chastised and obedient.

Travis finished his song. The camera faded back to the television host. Beynor lowered the volume.

Steven's cell phone rang. "There's room for improvement, David," Steven said to the man on the other end of the phone line, "but it's certainly an excellent beginning. What did Travis have to say? I see. Well, we'll talk more about it in the morning. I'll arrange for a copy of the video, so we can go over it, frame by frame, with everyone."

Steven signed off and turned his attention to Beynor.

"Is David happy, then?" Beynor asked.

"Very."

"And Travis?"

"Brooding," Steven said, "but when he realizes the success he's realized, he'll soon come out of his funk … yet again. I've run across his kind before. As soon as the money starts coming in, he'll be as passive as a pussy cat."

"I wonder," Beynor said.

"He hasn't beaten up anyone else lately, has he?"

"Not that I know of."

"Then, why the worried look?"

"I don't know," Beynor admitted. "A gut-feeling."

"Travis will be all right," Steven assured. He got out of the bed and walked across the thick rug to the desk near the fireplace. He opened the top drawer and took out a manila envelope which he brought back with him.

"I was going to save this until later, but you might as well have it now."

"What is it?"

"A gift," Steven said, sitting down on the edge of the bed.

"You've already given me quite a bit."

"And you usually don't protest nearly as much."

"Doing so, now, is supposed to make you think that I'm not trying to take advantage." Beynor grinned.

"Don't worry about taking advantage of me," Steven said. "I can fend for myself."

"Can I open this now?"

"Why not?"

Beynor opened the envelope, taking out the official-looking documents from inside. He read one, glanced at the others, and whistled softly.

"You deserve them," Steven smiled. "If it hadn't been for you, there wouldn't now be the corporation that's Travis Butcher."

"What did David and Travis have to say about my getting points?"

"Nothing," Steven said. "They had no chance. I made it a condition for my taking over the promotion. I doubt they would have made much of a fuss anyway. For some strange reason, they like you. They know, too, they would never have gotten to me without you."

"David has paid me for that already," Beynor reminded, "and quite well."   "Chicken feed!" Steven said. "If Travis hits it big, David will be spending that much money an evening on booze."

"Many thanks," Beynor said. He knew what he had in hand, remembering that Steven had once told him that if he played his cards right, he would be able to retire young. Well, this was one helluva good start. While Travis, David, and Steven were the chief stockholders, Beynor had just been handed a small but lucrative piece of the pie.

"Any strings I should know about that come attached to these?" Beynor asked.

"None," Steven replied. "With or without you, I'm still holding the majority. You can do with yours whatever you damned well please. Sell them tomorrow if you want."

Beynor put the stock certificates back in their envelope which he placed on the stand beside the bed. He scooted to make room for Steven. Steven didn't immediately join him.

"I'm not giving you those or anything else I have given you, or may yet give you, with any illusions about our relationship," Steven said. He walked away from the bed and to the small bar set-up in one corner. "I've long passed an age of believing in love that endures forever. Perhaps, I've even passed the point of believing in love, period. I know that it's not love that we have, here and now, nor will it probably turn into love in the future. I do want you to know, though, that I appreciate you for what you are and for what you've brought me. If the only way I can say thank-you is to provide a few gifts, stocks, bonds, money, and contacts, along the way, then I expect you to take them with no qualms. You're not dealing with a gullible innocent, here, who doesn't know the ropes. I've been around the block more than a few times and can see everything clearly. One should always get a return on one's investment. I've always gotten one from mine, and you had best get one from yours. Do you understand what I'm trying to say?"

"Yes," Beynor said, knowing that he *did* understand and hoping that Steven would know that it wasn't something Beynor admitted merely to patronize.

"You would make it sooner or later by yourself, in whatever route you decided to choose," Steven said. He had filled two glasses with ice and Scotch. He brought them back to the bed. "I'm just letting you get your independence sooner than you might have done, otherwise. When you're young, it's hell depending on others. When you're old, it's hell trying to enjoy the money you've worked so long and so hard to get."

Beynor took the offered glass.

"I like you," Steven said, sipping from his glass but still not sitting on the bed. "Notice I said *like* and not love. It's very easy to love someone…for a second, a minute, a day, a year. It's very hard to actually like someone."

"The feeling is mutual," Beynor replied.

Steven eyed Beynor curiously, as if trying to decide whether the statement rang true. Unable to make that determination, he continued.

"It's not just the sex. That could end today, or tomorrow, and it wouldn't make any difference. Oh, don't get me wrong. Certainly, I would miss it, but it wouldn't make my feelings for you any different."

Steven went back to the bar, refilled his glass. He turned back to Beynor.

"Oh, shit! I don't know really how to say any of this. I just hope I succeed in getting a little of it into your hard skull."

"My skull isn't the part of my body presently the hardest," Beynor protested.

A buzzer sounded. Steven looked at Beynor and frowned.

"Late-night visitor?" Beynor asked.

"Who in the hell is it at this hour?" Steven asked, mainly to himself. He asked the same question, in exactly the same tone of voice, into the intercom.

"Reggie Pierce," the voice came in reply. "May I come up?"

"Sure, Reggie," Steven said. He pushed the button by the phone that released the elevator to proceed to the penthouse. He turned back to Beynor. "Well, this is certainly a surprise."

"Should the name ring a bell?" Beynor asked. He watched as Steven got his robe and put it on.

"If you don't know the name, you'll recognize the face and body. A couple of years back, you couldn't find an underwear advertisement in any of the slick magazines, or on any Times Square billboard, that didn't have Reggie's physique staring down at you. Since then, he's moved behind the camera at *Before Dawn*."

"The magazine?"

"There hasn't been a recent photo in its pages that Reggie hasn't personally overseen. It's an indication of his work that sees his magazine with the highest circulation in the entertainment industry."

Steven went to the door, wanting to be in the living room, not bedroom, to greet Reggie when the elevator opened.

"Wait a few minutes and then join us," he said over his shoulder to Beynor. "You and Reggie should really get to know one another. If he hadn't made it so big in his own fields, he could have offered you some competition in yours."

Steven left the bedroom. Beynor slipped out from between the sheets and went to the mirror. As usual, he was pleased with what he saw reflected back. However, he didn't stop to play Narcissus this time around. His hair wasn't combed, but the tousled look was decidedly flattering. He left it as it was, got his Steven-issued robe from the floor where he'd previously dropped it, and went in to join the two men now in the living room.

Reggie had put his six-foot frame on the couch and was already drinking the glass of single-malt Scotch with which Steven had greeted him. His quick eye spotted Beynor in the bedroom doorway before Steven did.

"This is Beynor, Reggie," Steven said. "Beynor, this is Reggie Pierce."

"Hi," Beynor said and nodded, en route to the drink Steven had prepared in anticipation of his arrival.

Reggie had operated for so many years, both in front of, and behind, a lens, that his mind pretty much perpetually acted like a camera. Within seconds of seeing Beynor, he had selected several of the "right" poses that would best do Beynor justice, had mentally transfixed those poses onto 8 x 10 glossy photo paper, and had selected which of those would be best for a layout in *Before Dawn*.

Beynor took his glass and sat in one of the chairs opposite Reggie. Steven took up position in one next to him.

Beynor took the chance to better survey the newcomer. Steven had certainly been right about one thing. Beynor did recognize the face and the body, although, without Steven's hints, he would have probably been at a loss as to just why they should seem so familiar.

"It has been awhile, Reggie," Steven said.

Reggie stretched his legs languidly; the cloth at the crotch of his pants was on the move.

"I hope you don't mind the hour I chose to drop-by, in that I obviously seem to have gotten you both up from bed," Reggie said. He had the kind of smile that cameras loved. It was all white teeth and dimpled cheeks. It was all decidedly "all-American boy". His light-brown hair was long but not too long and feathered over his ears and forehead. He wore an outfit which would have made him acceptable in any leather bar, even though none of what he wore was leather. Beynor wasn't really sure what the material was; it might even have been faded brown denim, but it came off as very expensive. Whatever it was, it molded easily and sexily to a body that obviously hadn't lost much of its excellence over the years. Although he wasn't in front of the cameras very often anymore, Reggie's absence, there from, was the camera's loss.

"Is it late?" Steven asked.

"I was taking a chance, of course, that you would be awake at least long enough to watch your latest find do his thing on the tellie."

Suddenly, Steven suspected why Reggie was there. If right, it would almost assure Travis another bump up the ladder of success. However, it wasn't well to count one's chickens before they were hatched, especially in this instance, where there were obstacles. And, of course, Steven might possibly have misconceived the reason for the visit. Reggie could well have other reasons for being there, completely unassociated with Travis Butcher. Steven would wait and let it all come out in Reggie's own sweet time. In the back of his mind, however, he couldn't help feeling that even if Reggie had come to put Travis in *Before Dawn*, the complications of making that happen might be too great to surmount. Reggie, a well-known masochist, was well known for recruiting his models, male and female, to render services other than just modeling. Steven was wary of risking his investment in Travis by subjecting the young singer to Reggie's particular form of perversion — at least this early in the game. It wasn't because Steven feared Travis would come to any physical harm. The young man had enough judo and karate lessons behind him to make him invincible in a fight with anyone except a professional in the art of self-defense. It was Reggie's well-being that Steven would be worried about. Any beating Travis gave Reggie wouldn't be ruled or controlled by an inherent knowledge by Travis of the limits tolerated, or respect of any "safe word". Reggie might find that hard to understand. He might even be silly enough to think that Travis's professed heterosexuality was merely a promotional ploy. Either misconception could end up one helluva big mistake.

"Did you like the performance?" Beynor asked.

Reggie wondered how Steven had suddenly lucked out with two of the most exciting men Reggie had come across in a long time.

"Quite impressive," Reggie said. His statement was partly in reply to Beynor's query and partly in appreciation of Beynor's good looks.

"You'll agree, then, that he's 'the' next new rock star on the horizon?" Steven asked.

"Possibly," Reggie was noncommittal. "His delivery definitely needs a bit more polish, and you certainly should have a talk with make-up. When you've a face like his, you're defeating your purpose by using all that gunk to cover it up."

"I've already made similar notes," Steven admitted.

"And I suppose you've already guessed why I'm here," Reggie said. There was very little point in delaying the obvious.

"Shall I take a guess, then?"

"I was thinking of putting Travis on the cover of *Before Dawn*," Reggie said, rather than let any obvious guessing begin.

Steven's glass stopped en route to his mouth. The *cover* of *Before Dawn* was more than he could have ever hoped for.

"Of course, we'd back it up with a couple of shots, and an editorial, inside," Reggie continued. "I was thinking of maybe even using him for one of my famously artsy-fartsy frontals."

"I couldn't go for the frontals, Reggie," Steven said.

Curiously, Reggie eyed Steven, wondering why not. Even Beynor saw the potential for Travis's career. It was very seldom *Before Dawn* used any unknown on its cover. Why object to an artistic in-good-taste frontal, either? Other such tastefully shot nudes had appeared in *Before Dawn* and in other respectable high-gloss magazines. Travis certainly seemed to have the body for it.

"Surely, the boy isn't shy?" Reggie commented slyly. "What better way to exploit his bisexual image than by giving his audience a glimpse of just what they, men and women, have scheduled for their wet dreams?"

"Confidentially, Reggie, he's not well enough hung for one of your magazine's tasteful frontals," Steven said finally.

"Oh," Reggie said with a resigned sigh, accepting Steven's explanation without questioning it. "A real pity, in that I had expected more from the way he looked this evening in those tight pants."

"The body is real; the basket was slightly improvised."

It would have been ridiculous to keep that from Reggie who more than anyone knew the advantages of getting space in *Before Dawn*.

"It was a very good job of padding," Reggie commented in passing. "Congratulations in having fooled a pro."

"It's not that what he has isn't adequate," Steven said. "As a matter of fact, it's more than adequate. Unfortunately, you know an audience likes to think that its idol has elephantine dimensions."

"You're right, of course," Reggie admitted. Penis enhancement was done all of the time in the music world, and in the theater. One sex idol, with an exceptionally small dick had gyrated his way to the top with a basket that was two-thirds buckshot. "I'm glad you told me, now, to save me from major disappointment later."

"I just want you to know what you'd be getting," Steven said. "And while we're at it, I might go one step further, in that you shouldn't expect any reciprocal sex from Travis, either."

"Lordy! Hung like an ant and celibate as well?"

"Straight."

"Is it true, then, that he beats up homosexuals?" Reggie asked and actually licked his lips.

"Try to remember, Reggie, that Travis is neither homosexual nor knowledgeable about the pain-enhancing games of the kind you play. He gives pain not to provide for anyone's pleasure, even his own, but rather to dole out punishment. With his expertise in karate, alone, I'm afraid what might happen if he actually comes across someone who actually enjoys being beaten on, and assumes Travis would know a safe word even if he heard one."

"I'm a big boy, Steven," Reggie said, "although I am touched by your concern."

"No frontals and no sex," Steven said. "I'm afraid you would come out disappointed on both counts."

"Should I, I wonder, withdraw my offer, then?" Reggie mused.

"Listen," Steven said, leaning forward to give an impression of talking man-to-man. "You and I know that someone with Travis's potential is going to get to the top with or without coverage (or un-coverage) in *Before Dawn*. He may not get to the top quite as quickly, but he will get there. Now, is your magazine a publication that indicates the pulse of the times, or is it merely a tool you utilize to satiate your own carnal lusts?"

Reggie laughed. It was deep-throated, masculine, and portrayed real amusement.

"Shit, Steven, let's not be too dramatic. Actually, *Before Dawn* is just a little bit of both. Is either so bad?"

"It's bad if you let the latter override the former, as you might be tempted to do. Yours is an entertainment magazine. After tonight, can you deny that Travis is destined for his place in the entertainment world?"

"So, what, if anything do *you* propose?"

"You know exactly what I propose. Before our little chat, you thought he was good enough for a *Before Dawn* cover. Surely, he has just as much potential for that, now, as when you first arrived."

"What if we compromise?" Reggie suggested. "How about I give him a few non-frontal pictures on inside, and a small editorial, but no cover?"

"How about, you give him the cover, too, and I'll give you a model who'll do justice to any artsy-fartsy frontal you'd like to include in your magazine?"

"Go on."

"Beynor, here, is hung like a horse. Plus, he has the body and face that'll have your readers creaming their pants and panties."

Beynor settled deeper into his chair. He put his empty liquor glass on the end table and folded his arms across his chest. Both Steven and Reggie's eyes were focused on him. Each awaited his reaction. He gave them nothing, used not to showing his emotions. Whether or not he was flattered by what had just been proposed depended mainly upon two things: whether Reggie would agree; whether Beynor could see any real advantage in it for himself.

"I must admit that's an interesting counter proposal," Reggie said. Since he had been thinking of bringing up some similar variation on that idea, he was glad Steven had done so first, since it was no secret that Steven and Beynor had something going on between them.

"We *are* an entertainment magazine," Reggie said. "I'm just wondering if our readers would be ready for the caption explaining Beynor's occupation in the entertainment community."

"Write him up as my personal assistant."

"Let me think about it, will you, Steven?" Reggie said. He put his empty glass on the coffee table and got up. Of course, he could have given his decision, then and there, but it would be better to let Steven think that Reggie wasn't quite as anxious to do as asked as he really was. "In the meantime, you might want to check with Beynor, here, to see just how he feels about baring his all to a fairly substantial *Before Dawn* readership."

"You don't want another drink?" Steven asked, standing. He knew he had the cover story pretty much cinched, and he had seen, from the get-go, the magnetism Beynor had exerted on Reggie. Beynor would be able to handle Reggie, even through any S&M games that might result. No doubt, Beynor had run into several people in the past who wanted what Reggie wanted: a great deal of sex combined with some minor physical abuse. Beynor would know just how far to go without going past that point where the pain overrode Reggie's pleasure. Beynor would respect any safe word … where Travis wouldn't have had a clue.

"I really have to go," Reggie said. "I'll let you know, one way or the other, within the next couple of days."

Beynor stood and shook Reggie's hand. Both had firm grips. And Beynor, as well as Reggie, had made his decision, since Steven and Beynor had already agreed that Steven and Beynor's relationship couldn't boil hot forever. Having sex with Reggie might actually be fun, and any resulting layout in *Before Dawn*—even a nude one—was good exposure, with some possibly definite networking advantages. Firstly, of course, Beynor would have to put definition to just what Reggie expected of him. There had been more than passing reference to S&M. Beynor would want to know just how much of either/or was required, to what intensity, and who, for sure, would be on the receiving end of the stick (literally and figuratively).

Beynor and Steven walked Reggie to the elevator. When the man was gone, Beynor and Steven returned to the living room.

"It'll be a good way for you to meet some other important people," Steven said. "You see the advantages in that as well as I do, yes? No matter what anyone tells you, a lot of what you get in this world depends upon who you know."

"I'll look damned ridiculous in comparison to some of the professional models bound to be on display in the magazine with me."

"Who in the hell are you trying to kid?" Steven said.

"Maybe, we should go to bed and sleep on it," Beynor suggested with a smile.

This is just what they did.

CHAPTER SIX

Sally knew where Travis kept the extra key to his apartment; he'd used it once when she'd been with him; about which he'd likely forgotten, or he would have moved it long ago. It was in a small plastic envelope, like the ones used by coin or stamp collectors, buried about an inch, at ten-o'clock position, in the soil of the circular pot, just to the left of the elevator door, which, also, contained one of the management's many exuberant ficuses.

She surprised herself by feeling guilty when she unlocked his door and stepped inside. Maybe, that was because she knew Travis wasn't there; nor had Travis given her permission to stop on by. Steven Gladson had lined Travis up for a big upcoming performance at the stadium, and there were lots of rehearsal times, one of which had been scheduled for that very moment.

Once fully inside, the door shut behind her, Sally remembered just why she had been there only a few times, preferring that they end their evenings, not to mention begin and end their fucking, in *her* condo. Travis's place was a typical man-den, with no visible indication of a female's touch; which, under the circumstances, was something Sally was glad to see, because she strongly suspected Travis was having an affair. She was where she was because she'd come with every intention of ferreting out whatever evidence he or his clandestine cunt had left on his premises.

The only thing she saw so far was his discarded clothes and dirty underwear, what looked like a bath towel that he might have brought with him from a shower; an Army blanket was half on and half off the couch; on the coffee table, there was a copy of the *Before Dawn* magazine, with Travis on its cover, sharing space with a bowl of half-eaten popcorn with enough carelessly scattered kernels to likely feed a family of six; his small tabletop had an old pizza carton and a residual smell that indicated the last of the pizza had neither been eaten nor taken to safety within the refrigerator. Both sides of the sink were piled high with odorous dirty dishes buzzed by several flies. There was a toppled box of cereal on the counter adjacent to the sink, individual pieces of the spilled product looking like part of the décor. The refrigerator was pretty much empty, except for an almost-depleted jar of peanut butter, a moldy piece of some unidentifiable "something", and a carton of milk which—Good God!— had gone bad. All pretty much indicative of the why Travis, in the past, had so often accepted Sally's invites for a decent meal, and a fuck at her place, in exchange for sex.

The lone picture on the living-room wall, a nondescript land-scape that could have depicted any rural scene from pretty much any place in the world, didn't look anything like what Sally would have expected, even though Travis had never expressed any particular interest whatsoever in art other than what was associated with the music industry. There were no personal pictures, period. Not that Sally would expect Travis to want a picture of an abusive father anywhere near, but she found it strange he didn't at least have a picture of his mother, or even of himself with a buddy or two.

She centered in on the couch, if just because it seemed the most likely place, at least in that room, for any spontaneous fucking to oc-cur. Travis really wasn't the type of lover who would swipe a table-top clean with his arm to screw someone there, and the only time he and Sally had fucked on the floor had been at her insistence.

Up close, the couch's upholstery was stained so much that it was impossible to tell which of it had resulted from body fluids. She shuddered to think what would have resulted had she thought to bring a black light; probably so much glowing spent/stale cum from past tenants that it would have been impossible to figure out Travis's contribution to the mix.

She did pull out each of the three couch cushions, looking for any stray condom wrapper, albeit reminding herself to be sure and wash her hands before she next got her fingers anywhere near her face. All she found was a dime and three pennies, a gum wrapper, a paper clip, three candy-like beads that could once have been breath mints, more popcorn kernels, and a very large, very flattened, wad of lint.

His bathroom didn't yield anything suspicious, either. All of the medicines in the cabinet were generic, or his prescription (the latter for sinus congestion). It was only his shaving gear and after-shave lotion on the counter beside the dirty sink, nothing to provide incriminating evidence of a woman's need for powders and lotions and potions and … only one toothbrush and a tube of toothpaste squeezed flat in its center.

Pausing in the bathroom doorway, on the verge of a detailed go-through of the only remaining room—the bedroom—she paused momentarily to wonder if she hadn't, somehow, been mistaken that Travis was sleeping with someone else. It was looking more and more possible that his recent lethargy as fuck-master, even as regarded his apparent disinterest in even providing an occasional backhand, might very well just be the result of the hours he spent, like now, rehearsing for his upcoming major gig, and not because he'd expended most of his energy and sperm in screwing some slut.

Sally remained disconcerted that she somehow even seemed to care that he was or wasn't screwing around with anyone else, as if there wasn't plenty of candidates in the music pool of wanna-be artists needing a meal or two and willing to put out for it. It wasn't as if Sally were an old hag or something. She was young, pretty, had money, and was a damned good fuck, if she did say so herself — and she did say so. Self-admittedly, her pique might well be the result of her being the one who usually said a relationship was over and done. Not that Travis had actually said their relationship was finished, but there was just something hinky about him lately, his fuck sessions, fewer and farther between, definitely depleted of energy, as if he'd expended a lot of it elsewhere before he'd ever gotten around to screwing her. She liked to think she didn't miss his hitting her around, quite as much, nor his doing as much physical damage as he had in the past, and she had every conceivable reason to use his onset of sexual lethargy as an excuse, as good as any, to drop his sorry ass by the wayside, but there was something that had kept her clinging when every instinct told her that clinging, in any way, to Travis and to his emotional instability and volatility was the last thing she should be doing. That she was hanging on, even where she was at the moment, doing what she was doing, indicated a psychological something in her character that, while recognized, wasn't something she liked, wanted, or appreciated. She had enjoyed her free-wheeling independence for a good long while, and that she, now, for some unfathomable reason, couldn't let go of this damaged young man and all of his baggage, was like a ball and chain attached to her leg not letting her get on with her life as she had in the past.

Nevertheless, in for a penny, in for a pound. She'd come this far, only scrutiny of his the bedroom left—the place where sexual she-nanigans seem most likely to occur if they occurred—and she had no real desire to make a return trip, any time soon, to this undeniable sty, to conduct additional investigation she could very well take care of, here and now. So, she circled the room with yet another lone picture on its wall, this one, a reprint of undoubtedly some famous painting of a genuinely somber Renaissance gentleman even less "Travis" than was the living-room's painted landscape.

More discarded clothes: all men's. No female clothing in the closet that smelled of old socks, either. Nothing under the bed but a pair of soiled underwear and a pair of jeans paint-stained with a color Sally didn't recognize from any of the walls.

When there was only beneath-his-mattress left to explore, she almost didn't bother. It seemed inconceivable that anyone, in this day and age, so exposed to movies and television, would ever fathom concealing anything in a place so obvious, usually the first locale "tossed" in any kind of fishing expedition or raid. Nonetheless, her brother had been just so stupid, keeping his nudie magazines, so se-questered, although the ill-hidden cache had early been discovered by his mother and his father who found it "healthy", and by Sally who had never, then, or since, fathomed her brother's seeming penchant for women with breasts so big as to seem to threaten their stability in even managing to walk.

She found two magazines beneath Travis's mattress. Not porn, but one and the same edition of the *Before Dawn* on which Travis, shirtless, was on the cover; both copies were decidedly dog-eared and looking definitely the worst for wear. Why they were there, saved and concealed, when there was a pristine copy of the same, on the coffee table in the living-room, was a puzzle Sally didn't ponder until she had dropped the mattress back into place, prepared to leave. Only in retrospect, did she retrieve both copies for closer inspection, thumb through each separately, and find the same two pages in each inexplicably plastered together with the same kind of spermal glue which had, likewise, cemented several of her brother's favorite pages in his nuddie-magazine collection.

Of course, she'd seen a copy of this magazine before, but remembering its contents to the point where she could isolate the stuck pages in question remained illusive. Trying gently to ease the pages apart with a fingernail, to reveal the temporary secret, saw her doing nothing but tearing the paper.

She replaced the two much-used and abused magazines, similarly as situated as she remembered originally finding them, and retreated to the couch in the living room and to the magazine on the coffee table in front of her. She flipped through the pages, passing the picture and write up of a young ballerina presently the reigning star of the ballet season, and the story of an attractive debutante who was making her movie debut in a much ballyhooed horror movie, and the article on the decidedly beautiful female artist who had just sold a painting for close to a quarter of a million dollars — all possibly candidates for the masturbatory fantasies of a hot and horny Travis — until she came to the advertisement for Fendi Pour Homme Acqua, the new fragrance for men, directly opposite the full-page nude frontal black-and-white photo of Steve Gladson's aide, Beynor Wilden, mainly lost within a ghostly background of seemingly leafless primeval trees whose shadows somehow concealed him and most of his penis while making the latter appear even larger than its already obviously impressive reality.

CHAPTER SEVEN

Duncan Temple, though gay, wrote in a he-man style that complemented his rugged good looks.

He had wanted to write as far back as high school, but he had found himself too involved with sports, the same when at university, to do any serious writing. He was good in sports. He even enjoyed them. It helped his image, too, that anyone who participated in them was usually assumed a real man, few suspecting Duncan actually preferred men. He'd enlisted in the Army, because a real man went into the military. A real man served his country. So what that Duncan was still in Basic Training when he fucked his first fellow soldier… in the shower…one night? There were other soldiers, fucked and doing the fucking, over the next three years, but no one ever seemed to suspect, and Duncan had been honorably discharged, risen to the rank of Sergeant (E-5).

After which, he began to write. He had the germ of his first novel in mind, but he didn't yet have the writing skills he needed to write it. Instead, he turned to writing magazine articles. He could have ended up doing that for the rest of his life if not for one drunken evening having accidently stumbled into a leather bar. He liked the people there—strong, rugged, and masculine. He liked the sex to which he was introduced in the back room—rough and heavy-handed, that left him satisfied and satiated. He wove those experiences into his first novel that had not only shocked a lot of people but thrust him, overnight, into the role of a prime player, with crossover readership, on a literary stage where book buyers were becoming more and more difficult to come by.

His latest and fourth book, *Timothy*, was based even more on his life, and, like books one through three, it had been opted for the movies. By this time in his career, Duncan had enough box-office success behind him to demand, and get, complete say as to who played him in the film version. He wanted Beynor Wilden, in no way influenced by a long forgotten glowing description once given by Reggie Pierce as to how Beynor had tied Reggie to a bed and, then, beaten him to climax with a Gucci belt. As a matter of fact, Reggie so often related such tales of his latest finds that Duncan had really paid very little attention, at the time, even when Reggie's account of Beynor had been more glowing than usual. When Reggie had even suggested that Duncan and Beynor get together for a little S&M fun of their own, Duncan had only smiled. Reggie was always suggesting get-togethers with some young stud, or the other, for a really good time. The suggestions rarely came to anything but suggestions. Reggie was usually way too busy with his latest find to share. Besides, at the time, Duncan was, as usual, busy writing and talking shop with movie people.

Rather, Duncan picked Beynor as the sole result of another evening, among many, that he spent enduring the frustrations of one more casting call. The movie was scheduled to begin shooting in a week, and Duncan hadn't given his okay to anyone for the lead. He and the production crew had spent days going through a gamut of good-looking men whose names had been submitted for consideration. The big-name star the studio had originally pushed had been vehemently vetoed by Duncan, and film executives were still foaming at the mouths because of it, but Duncan didn't care. It had taken him years, and three movie adaptations, none of which he had really liked, despite their popularity with movie-going audiences, to get him into a position of power, where his contract with the movie studio was tipped in his favor, and he wasn't going to give an inch. At a time when the movie industry was contemplating yet another slump, it was hard to find material that could pull in money at the box office. In order to get Duncan's latest best-seller under its wing, the studio had paid through the teeth, as well as assigned carte blanche as far as Duncan's approval of the cast. Graciously, he had stood aside and let the casting department fill most of the supporting roles, but he refused to let them assign the lead to someone just because that someone was the producer or director's latest fuck. If he hadn't found the right person to play Timothy, then he wouldn't have allowed filming to proceed; for the first time in his life, he wasn't so strapped for cash that he needed to compromise.

He had entered his living room on that fateful day, with the sounds of irate movie people still ringing in his ears. He had made himself a stiff drink and sprawled his six-foot-two body on the five-foot-ten-inches of available rented-house couch. He had, then, picked up the copy of *Before Dawn* on the coffee table. It was while thumbing through the magazine that he found Beynor Wilden and knew he *had* to play Timothy. The name "Beynor", which identified the young man in the photo layout and in the supplementary captions, as well as "Photographs by Reggie Pierce", never had him make the Beynor-Pierce-Gucci-S&M connection. Though, he immediately gave Reggie a call. Reggie was out.

He had tried, again, and left a message with the answering service. Then, he took the copy of *Before Dawn* into the bedroom, leaving it open on the bed while he stripped for a shower.

In only his Jockey shorts, he compared his reflection with the picture of the man on the slick pages of the magazine. They weren't the same. Duncan had short-cropped brown hair; Beynor's hair was longer and blond. Duncan had little hair on his chest, belly, and legs. Duncan estimated himself at least two inches taller than Beynor and probably five years older. Yet, whatever those differences, they didn't matter; when Duncan looked at Beynor Wilden, he *saw* Timothy Templar.

Reggie returned Duncan's call, during which he reminded Duncan that Reggie had met Beynor in a gay bar, having gone with him back to Reggie's place for S&M games, the details of which had already been related to Duncan, in some delicious detail, once upon a time.

"So, you're *finally* interested?" Reggie asked.

"Definitely, I'd like to meet him, but not for sex."

"You're kidding, right?"

"Specifically, I'm wondering if he can act."

"As in pretend he's having a good time, whether or not he is?"

"As in…can he speak in words of more than one-syllable? As in…can he memorize script and manage to repeat it?"

"Why don't I hook the two of you up, then you tell me?" Reggie suggested.

"When?"

"It might be difficult to do really soon, in that he's presently pretty much tied up with the promotion of the latest up-and-coming rock star, Travis Butcher, and Travis's back-up group *The Meat*."

"Never heard of them."

"That's Travis on the cover of the magazine you found Beynor in," Reggie reminded.

"Oh!" Duncan only vaguely remembered a bare-chested young man, somewhat attractive, on the cover.

"How about sometime the week after next?"

"How about sooner?"

"Why the sudden hurry?" Reggie asked with a laugh.

"He looks right to me for the part of Timothy in the new movie. I'd like to meet up and make sure. We hope to have casting over and done by the end of *this* week."

"In that case, I'll see what I can do." Reggie realized what a plum Beynor would have if he could get the part. Some awfully big names had already tried and failed. "No promises, though, since *Travis and The Meat* have this big thing going down at the stadium next week; it's keeping everyone damned busy."

"Just see what you can do."

Reggie called back the next day. Beynor had agreed to meet with Duncan on the same night as Travis's scheduled stadium performance. It was quite impossible for Beynor to get away before then. Duncan wished he could make it sooner, but caved to the inevitable. When Reggie hung up, Duncan called the studio and told them he'd found the person he wanted to play Timothy. The executives were so overjoyed that they were going to be able to stick to their original shooting schedule that they didn't even make a fuss when Duncan told them he wouldn't be able to bring the unknown actor around for their look-see before late next week. If it turned out Beynor couldn't act for shit, Duncan would make those needed apologies and explanations when he had to.

CHAPTER EIGHT

Sally never really had any pressing need to resort to sex with needy young men enticed to put out for a free meal. Early on, she had merely discovered that was easy to do and convenient, since she had money to spend. It remained a business transaction, and, therefore, didn't get her involved in messy personal relationships. She was a genuine fan of the music business and enjoyed being with and around the people in it, no matter what echelons they'd achieve or would achieve. The sex was enjoyable, since she liked sex, and most men would have jumped into bed with her for less than a six-course meal that included liquor and chateaubriand.

Except all of that had changed, and she blamed Travis, although she had dumped his sorry ass by the wayside when she'd discovered that he was not only an abusive lover but a decided pervert in his obvious penchant for jacking-off over pictures of a naked Beynor Wilden. If the mystery remained as to how he could have fucked Sally so damned well and still waste his cum on some guy posed on an inanimate glossy magazine page (bisexuality?), the fact remained that he had screwed her so well, so many times, that his fucks had become the baseline upon which she now judged every hump that came her way. That wouldn't have been nearly as bad as it was if there had at been at least one fuck lately, come her way, that she could have been satisfied was superior to even one of the screws Travis had delivered.

Before Travis (BT), she had always enjoyed sex with Robby Timsdale. When she'd first got together with him, he'd already been a big name in the music business, making more than enough money to put food on his own plate and live in a decidedly plush penthouse with the kind of four-poster bed Marie Antoinette likely enjoyed at Versailles. They hadn't hooked up because of any other reason than that they'd immediately been sexually attracted to each other, Robby having chosen her to join him over younger and more eager girls who flocked around him and his other Riotous band members pretty much on a 24/7 basis. When Sally had returned to him, just the other evening, at the Powhatchet Indian Casino, where he was headlining, it went without saying that she would be the gal who he would nail to his dressing-room closet door during half time, and that's just the way things had turned out.

If their sex wasn't as good as Sally remembered, it wasn't as if Robby seemed to notice any difference. He was ramming his hard cock in and out of her like a piston gone wild, as he always did when approaching climax, his face buried against the nape of her neck while his mantra — "God, baby, you are so, so good ... so, so tight!" — reassured her that whatever she found a little off, by way of what they were doing, wasn't anything that he was noticing at the time. If the final placement of his stiff dick deep inside her, and his resulting animalistic groans, in low-moan accompanied to the spurting expulsions of his hot seed from his large balls into his condom, managed to provide Sally with the orgasm she usually accompanied him with, there were orgasms and then there were orgasms.

"Holy shit," he said, pulled his cock out, grabbed a handful of tissue with which to wipe it off before sticking it back into its impressive lumping of the faded crotch of his blue jeans, "I just hope you've left me energy enough to go out and perform the second part of my concert."

He buttoned up his fly, checked his reflection in his vanity-table mirror, used more tissue to wipe sweat off his forehead and neck, and turned back to Sally who had finally finished straightening her clothes.

"You planning on sticking round after the show, honey?" he asked. His smile was wide in a face more handsome than a lot of people would ever find Travis Butcher.

"Never know," she said noncommittally. She wasn't sure she wanted any follow-up disappointing fucks to make her realize all the more that her sex life hadn't been anywhere as exciting as it had been with Travis, even after Travis had started taking to wasting a lot of his spunk on pictures of Beynor Wilden.

"Feel free to stick around in here, have a beer, even take a shower," he said. "By the time I'm finished with my set, I'll have this cock of mine back into boner-status and ready for seconds."

He gave her a quick kiss and, then, answered the knock on the door that informed it was time for him to get his ass back on stage. After which, he was gone, and Sally plopped down into a chair to try and figure out what in the hell was wrong with her life, these days, and just how and why Travis was as assuredly as responsible for the fuck-up as night was likely to follow the day.

CHAPTER NINE

From the minute Beynor walked into the hotel lobby, Duncan wasn't seeing Beynor Wilden but Timothy Templar come to life.

Seated in the lounge, the two hit it off immediately, getting friendlier by the minute until interrupted by an incoming call on Beynor's cell phone. He was more than tempted not to answer, although he did.

"Beynor?" Steven Gladson queried from the other end of the line. *Who else would it be answering Beynor's phone?*

"So how did the concert go?" Beynor asked.

"Listen, buddy," Steven said, his voice strained but controlled, "I know you're with Duncan Temple, and I know what the meeting can mean for you. I want you to know that I wouldn't ask you to leave there if this wasn't important."

"Something wrong?"

"I can't tell you what over the phone, but we need you back here at the stadium as quickly as possible. Just you, Beynor. Whatever you do, don't bring Duncan." Toward the end, his voice had faded as he'd apparently pulled away from the mouthpiece to say something to someone somewhere on the other end of the line. It returned, full-force, when he said, "Please, come as quickly as possible."

The phone went dead. Beynor continued holding it for several seconds, thinking there might be something more, but there wasn't. He looked to Duncan who was eyeing him curiously.

"What?" Duncan asked.

"That was Steven Gladson?" Beynor said.

"The concert of *Butcher and The Meat* not going as expected."

"A bit of a glitch," Beynor admitted, "and I'm afraid I'm needed. I do hope you know that I wouldn't hurry off if the circumstances didn't warrant it."

"Shall I wait here?"

"I think not. Why don't I call you when the crisis is over?"

Beynor left the hotel and walked the short distance to the stadium. He didn't know what he expected when he got there. From the tension in Steven's voice, Beynor thought maybe he would arrive with an accompanying fanfare of police sirens, police cars, and policemen. There was nothing, though, to indicate that less than an hour before the whole area had been jam-packed with the cars and the fans of the latest rock star to hit the music world. Steven's car, David's car, and Beynor's car were the only ones remaining in VIP parking.

The first two doors to the building that Beynor tried were locked. He was trying the third when he spotted Steven through the glass.

"Thank God, you're here!" Steven said, pushing open the door.

"You never did say what's wrong," Beynor reminded. "Leaving a person like Duncan Temple is sure to have *him* wondering."

"Right now, Duncan Temple isn't our biggest problem," Steven said. He took Beynor's arm and began propelling him down the hallway.

Beynor knew the route being taken. He had been along it just that very morning with Travis, David, and Steven. Then, it had been at a more leisurely pace. There had been the loud sounds of the work crew erecting the stage and positioning equipment.

David waited for them at the exit leading from the stage to the back galleries.

"Thank God, you're here!" David greeted.

"Is he still in there?" Steven asked.

"He says he won't come out," David said, "and he won't say whether or not the kid is dead?"

"What kid?" Beynor asked.

"Christ, Steven! Didn't you tell him?" David turned to Beynor. "Travis may well have killed some gay groupie."

"We don't know that he has," Steven reminded. His voice had a strained calmness emphasized by a sudden tic in his left cheek.

"What if he *is* dead?" David asked. He made no pretense of hiding his fear; Beynor could smell it on the air.

Steven turned his full attention on Beynor and said, "He left the stage, after his performance. You know, we had the back room set up for him to wait in until the screaming mob left. Somehow, one of the groupies found him."

"A gay guy, for Christ's sake," David said. "It had to be one of the goddamned, fuckin' gay guys."

"When Travis didn't show at the car, we went looking. He was in the waiting room with the kid, is still in the waiting room with the kid, door locked, and neither is coming out."

"What in the fuck am I supposed to do about it?" Beynor asked.

"He asked for you," Steven said.

"For me? Why in the hell would he ask for me?"

"He's always had a *thing* for you, you know that," David said.

"You have to be kidding!" Beynor said.

"This is getting us nowhere," Steven interjected. "Right now, it really doesn't matter *why* Travis wants you, only that he's willing to talk to *someone*."

"He has possibly killed one homosexual, and you two have called in another? I somehow get the impression I'm playing the sacrificial lamb being led to the slaughter."

"We had no choice," Steven said. "All of us have too much tied up in this, at this point, to call in the police, unless we absolutely have to."

"If I go in there, and I'm not out in ten minutes, I suggest you call the police *and* an ambulance," Beynor said. "Unfortunately, I left karate lessons out of my hustling regimen."

Beynor walked the short distance down the hallway. He put his ear against the door and listened. He didn't hear a damn thing.

"Travis?" He waited for an answer but received none. "Travis?" he tried a second time. "It's Beynor. Open the door and let me in, why don't you?"

He expected a long drawn-out period of coaxing. He was surprised when Travis immediately opened the door, albeit just a crack.

"Where are they?" Travis hissed.

"Who?"

"Steven and David."

"They're just down the hall. Shall I call them?"

"Hell, no!" Travis opened the door wider. It was dark inside. Beynor took a deep breath and slipped into the darkness. The door closed and locked behind him.

"Isn't there a light in here?" Beynor asked, wanting to hear something, even if it was his own voice. He was surprised he sounded as calm as he did.

"He's not very pretty," Travis said. He spoke in a very low voice.

His eyes still not adjusted to the darkness, Beynor could make out absolutely nothing.

"Is he dead?" Beynor asked, almost afraid to hear the answer. He doubted very much that there was any way even Steven or David could cover up a murder.

"Why couldn't he leave me alone?"

"Turn on the lights, Travis," Beynor said.

"I don't want to see him," Travis said. "I hurt him pretty badly."

"Turn on the lights, Travis!" Beynor repeated in definite command.

Travis obliged. Beynor's eyes took a few seconds to adjust to the resulting glare.

"Oh, Christ!" he said. The kid was slumped in a bloody mass against one wall. His face, or what was seemingly left of it, was pure pulp. Beynor wondered how the kid had once looked. It was apparent that he had an excellent body just by the way the front of his blood-soaked shirt molded his torso.

Travis sat so his pale but still-handsome face was reflected by a mirror on one wall.

"They're mad, aren't they?" he asked.

Beynor didn't answer. He was over at the slumped kid's body, checking for a pulse. He thought he found a very weak one, just as he saw a bubble of blood pulsing where the flattened nose was.

"Do you know why they're mad?" Travis continued. "They're mad, because I've endangered their fucking dreams. Steven sees me as another big money-maker. David sees me as his ladder back to the big-time. No one really gives a shit about that poor kid over there or about me as a person."

"Bullshit!" Beynor said. "I do."

Travis gave him a funny little smile.

"I think maybe you do," Travis said finally. A sudden shiver convulsed his body. He clasped his arms over his chest. His torso was still bare from the live show. "What do we do now?"

"I take you home," Beynor said.

"And him?" Travis nodded toward the bloody heap beside which Beynor was kneeling.

"We let David and Steven take care of him," Beynor said. "They'll get him to a hospital or something."

"Is he dead?"

"By his looks, he should be," Beynor said. "However, I don't think so."

"Can I have your coat?" Travis asked. "I'm cold."

Beynor gave him the suede sports jacket Beynor had worn to the Duncan interview. Travis slipped it on while Beynor opened the door, stepped into the hallway, and beckoned to Steven and David who immediately hurried forward.

"I think the kid is still alive," Beynor said in whispered greeting. "You'd better get him a doctor, and fast, because he's looking pretty bad. I told Travis I'd take him home."

"I'm ready," Travis said "Can we go? I need a drink."

"Yes, for Christ's sake, take him home, "Steven said to Beynor. "Get him a drink, and don't lose sight of him. David and I will try to take care of this mess."

"Is your car in the VIP lot?" Travis asked once he and Beynor were in the hallway.

All the drive to Travis's apartment, Travis feigned sleep. Beynor did nothing to interrupt the ruse. After they were in Travis's apartment, Travis was the first to break the silence.

"God, I hope he'll be all right." Ironically, he actually sounded sincere.

"Shouldn't you have thought of that a little earlier?" Beynor asked.

"Yes, I suppose so," Travis admitted.

"Jesus, Travis," Beynor said with an audible expulsion of breath, "do you know what this does for you and your career if that kid dies?"

"He was homosexual," Travis argued as if sexual preference adequately rationalized all he had done.

"Christ, so is David, so is Steven," Beynor said, "and so, for that matter am I."

"You?"

"Oh, come on, Travis," Beynor said, sinking into the nearest chair. "You can't possibly tell me you didn't know."

"I guess I can't," Travis conceded.

"But just because I am, do you think that gives you the right to beat the shit out of me whenever you damned well feel like it?"

"You're different," Travis said. "You don't try to get into my pants every time you turn around."

"What if I told you I didn't try only because I was afraid of what you might do?"

"That's not true," Travis said, walking to stand closer to Beynor's chair. "It's not, is it?"

"It's not true," Beynor admitted.

"I knew that," Travis said with conviction.

"What *is* your problem, though, Travis?" Beynor asked finally.

"Problem?"

"Surely, you recognize that you *do* have one. Other men get accosted by homosexuals and find it easier just to say no than go into a rage."

"Why do the queers even ask?"

"You're not so stupid as to try and tell me you don't know that you hold out a vast appeal for members of your own sex, are you?" Beynor asked. "Steven has based a good deal of your public image along those lines. If you beat up every homosexual that has the hots for you, you'll end up destroying half your record-buying public."

"Do you find me attractive?" Travis asked.

Beynor wondered where that line of conversation would lead them. Travis stood before him, suede jacket open to reveal the young man's bared chest. The top button of his jeans was still open from the performance.

"And if I say yes, will David and Steven arrive to find me the next bloody body propped against the wall."

"You're big enough to handle yourself," Travis said.

"*Of course* I find you attractive," Beynor said. "I'm surprised you even had to bother asking."

"You've never said anything."

"Like, what would you have suggested I say?" Beynor asked. "You insist you're straight, and I've enough willing people around without trying to seduce those who are unwilling." He stood. "Are you afraid, Travis, that you might actually find out that you enjoy sex with other men?"

"I don't know," Travis admitted. "Sometimes, I…"

"Go on."

"I can talk to you, can't I, Beynor?" He went to the bar, poured himself a stiff glass of Scotch and drank it. "I've always thought that I could, anyway. You're somehow different from the others…from David…from Steven. I always feel comfortable around you."

"Do you beat gay men silly so they can't tempt you with sex any longer?"

"I don't know why I do it."

"How do you know you wouldn't enjoy them and it?" Beynor asked.

"I don't know," Travis confessed. "I think that's what disturbs me the most."

"Why not give it a try sometime, Travis?" Beynor suggested. "Have sex and, then, if you don't like it, beat the queer up."

"Homosexuality isn't natural," Travis said.

"By whose definition?" Beynor asked.

"By society's definition."

"How archaic," Beynor said with a helpless smirk. "Times are a changing, buddy. Gay marriage is legal. Do you know that half your teeny-bopping worshipers would laugh you off the face of the earth if they ever heard that bit of triteness coming out of your mouth?"

"Do you love all of the men with whom you've had sex," Travis asked.

"Christ, no!"

"You can have sex with someone … and not love them?'

"Love and sex, at least for me, Travis, have never been one and the same and never will."

"Could you have sex with me if I were willing?"

"Do you want to have sex with me, Travis? We don't have to play games, not the two of us."

"I've this need inside of me," Travis said. "I feel it every time I'm propositioned by a man. It's still there after I hit him. It was with me all of the while I was waiting for you to show up, after I'd beaten the poor kid senseless."

"Is it with you now?"

"Yes."

"You know in a fight between us, you would likely come out the winner."

"I wouldn't fight you," Travis said.

"How can you be sure? How can I be sure?"

"I never asked any of the others," Travis said. "They've asked me. There's a difference."

"I'm not sure I should be your first," Beynor said. "You'd do better with someone you really like."

"I like you."

"I mean *really* like."

"I *really* like you."

Beynor walked passed Travis to the window. Through the drawn curtains, the lights of the city could be seen. It was hard to imagine that a few hours ago he'd been part of those lights. Travis came to stand behind him. Beynor didn't move or turn.

"Besides, did you *really* like the first man *you* had sex with?" Travis asked.

"Let me tell you about the first man I ever had sex with," Beynor said, still looking out over the city. "He was old, and he was ugly, and he was a cripple. He didn't choose me. I chose him. Do you know why?" He turned to face Travis in the dimness. Half the teenage population of the world would have given anything to be in Beynor's shoes, as regards potential sex with Travis, and Beynor was hesitating. "I picked him, because I wanted my first homosexual experience to be thoroughly *unenjoyable*."

"Why?"

"How in the fuck should I know?" Beynor said loudly, stepping to widen the distance between them. "Maybe, it was because of the same reason you beat up on gays. Maybe, it was because if I was going to make my living selling my body, I wanted to prove to myself that I could get 'it' up for anyone. Maybe, I thought my first experience should be so distasteful that I would always, somehow, associate gay sex with something revolting. Maybe, by some twisted reasoning, I thought it was a way to assure myself that I would never fall in love with any *man*."

"Has it worked?"

"I've never loved," Beynor said, "a man or a woman, for whatever the reason."

"Not even Steven?"

"I enjoy Steven. I don't love him."

"I want you," Travis said. "I've wanted you from the beginning. When I first saw you, I knew it would come to this, one day. Everyone I beat up, I beat up because he tempted me when I always promised myself my first sex would be someone I chose, like you."

Beynor was glad the phone rang.

"That was Steven," he said when the short conversation was over and done. "The kid will live and is tucked safely away in a private facility to keep him and his story from the press. Hopefully a big pay-off will keep him and his story from the press."

The two, without additional talk, went to the bedroom.

CHAPTER TEN

"Christ, I love you so much," Travis whispered when it was over and done.

Beynor heard the words and tried to dismiss them. He had heard the same thing, whispered before, from hundreds of people. They had meant nothing, merely part of the mantra of all those who liked to fool themselves into believing they would never have sex with *anyone* unless love was involved. The words, as uttered by Travis, however, were not so easily dismissed. Beynor silently cursed Travis for even saying them. Beynor suspected that Travis was not speaking just to hear himself talk. Beynor was afraid that Travis meant what he said. Beynor did not want him to mean it. Travis needed to give his love to someone who would give him something in return. Beynor couldn't return love. Beynor could hardly help himself, so how could Travis expect him to help anyone else? And Beynor had no doubts that Travis, even now, needed help.

"It was so good," Travis said in a low voice, his breath warm against Beynor's ear.

Beynor found it hard to equate this muscular teddy-bear as the same sadistic monster who had bloodied the gay kid earlier in the evening. The conflicting personalities, apparently coexistent, within this one individual, were more than a little disconcerting. It was uncanny that someone who had bashed in one kid, because the kid was queer, could now be in bed with another man, certainly as queer if not more so than the first, and seemingly be so euphoric.

"See," Beynor said. "It wasn't all as bad as you feared and imagined?"

"It's just how I knew it would be," Travis said, "with you."

Beynor didn't like that insinuation, either. He didn't like what responsibility could be encased within it. Certainly, he didn't like whatever the insinuated emotional ties.

"Maybe, now, you'll be able to enjoy at least a few of the men who proposition you," Beynor said, "instead of beating up on all of them."

"No," Travis said, and Beynor felt the resulting stiffness of the body beside him.

"Don't be a fool, Travis!" Beynor said. "You've now surely seen that there's nothing wrong with any of this."

"It just wouldn't be the same with anyone else," Travis said. "I could never let sex be impersonal."

"All sex can give you an orgasm," Beynor reminded.

Travis turned his eyes toward one wall. There was a mirror there in which he could see their reflection on the bed.

"It just wouldn't be the same," he said. "Sex *is* personal."

"Sex is sex," Beynor insisted. "It isn't enhanced by unnecessary emotional involvement."

"How do you know?" Travis asked, turning his gaze back on his companion. "You've never had an emotional involvement, have you?"

"Listen, Travis," Beynor said. "You've taken a giant step forward, this evening. Really, you have. You've discovered that something you thought abhorrent wasn't abhorrent at all."

"You're wrong," Travis said, "if you think I, even once, suspected any of this would be any less enjoyable than it was."

"Then, why beat up that kid this evening?"

"*This* moment," Travis emphasized. "*Me and you.* Not me and some drooling sex-craved teenie-bopper queer."

"That's absurd!"

"Nothing, here, changed anything," Travis said. "I'm still not queer. I'm still not a faggot. This thing between you and me goes beyond banal phraseology."

Beynor felt the frustrations welling up inside him. He wanted somehow to be able to tell Travis that the young man's reasoning was all twisted. Yet, he knew he would never make Travis understand. What Travis probably needed was professional help. Then, again, there were plenty of people who probably thought Beynor needed a psychiatrist, too.

"Don't worry about it," Beynor said, seeing Travis would never understand. He wished otherwise, but he knew it was highly unlikely.

Travis just wasn't made out of whatever it was that allowed people, like Beynor, to go to bed without some kind of emotional attachment, other than pure lust. In order for Travis to have sex with anyone, like he just had, he had to care for them. He had to live by such rules and regulations, or his life would be even more chaotic.

"What happens if one day you kill someone?" Beynor asked.

"You mean one of those people who only want to have sex with me because I'm a star, and they can go back to their friends and boast they've made it with Travis Butcher of *Butcher and The Meat*?"

"I'll tell you what happens—you'll be put in prison for a very long time and likely have male-male sex there which won't see you quite as able to beat up whomever propositions you."

Beynor had his own rules and regulations he had sworn not to violate. One of those was that he would never—ever—love. He had come too far to begin operating by any other rulebook, now. Maybe, if he and Travis could have found each other earlier, things might have been different, but they couldn't be changed now. Certain things were already embedded too deeply within both of their characters.

"Don't be sad," Travis said.

Beynor couldn't help being sad. Travis was looking at him with such a knowing look, but really knew nothing, understood not a bit. Travis didn't understand what was going on inside Beynor, any more than he could understand the contradictory forces at play within his own body.

"I do like you," Beynor said. "Really."

"Then, I shall have to settle for just that, won't I?" Travis said, and Beynor wondered if, perhaps, he had been mistaken. Maybe, Travis really could see what it was all about.

"I wish it could be more but…"

"Shhhhh," Travis said.

Beynor knew a crossroads had been encountered, and he had chosen his pathway with no turning back. He would look back many times, in the future, to this particular moment, wondering how it would have been changed if he had just chosen to be more open to the possibility of love.

CHAPTER ELEVEN

"Okay, you two, let's try and make this look *real,*" the director said. "This is a very crucial point in the script, and we don't want the audience having any doubts about what's happening. Are you both ready?"

"Ready," Frasier Delaney and Beynor replied in unison.

Duncan stood silently on the sidelines, watching his novel being acted out before him. He was content. Beynor was the perfect Timothy and could even act. Even the studio and director had ended up admitting that casting him was perfect.

Somewhere in the studio, a buzzer sounded for silence. The slate board was shown to the camera's eye, and the director finally called for action.

"Cut!" the director said three takes later. "And print!"

"Finally good, was it?" Frasier asked.

"So good that we'll probably never get it past censors," Duncan said from the sidelines.

Frasier laughed, winked at Beynor. He was about to ask Beynor to join him for a cup of coffee, but his plan was interrupted. The girl who brought Beynor his robe nodded at the two men who had apparently been admitted to the stage immediately after shooting. Beynor got up off the bed and went to join them. Frasier, taking his own robe, went off for a coffee with Duncan.

Beynor moved through the equipment and took David's hand.

"It's been awhile, hasn't it?" he said and smiled.

"You don't look any different, what with upcoming movie stardom," David said. "I hear you're making the cover of *Before Dawn* this time around."

"Reggie shot the pictures last month," Beynor said. "He was upset that Travis had postponed *his* latest session, by the way."

"Travis is kept pretty busy, these days," David said. "I think we've got Reggie penciled in on the calendar for sometime next week."

"Reggie will be happy to hear that," Beynor said. "He's really a bit worried about making his deadline."

"Do you know Harry Taxim?" David asked.

"I don't believe so."

"Beynor, Harry," David introduced the man with him. "Harry, Beynor. Is there somewhere more private, Beynor, where we can talk?"

Beynor looked at his watch, noticing that there *was* time and leading the two men to his dressing room in one of the trailers out back.

"Can I get either of you a drink?" Beynor asked.

"A Scotch for me, if you have it," David said. "Harry?"

"Scotch is fine."

Beynor poured three, gave his guests theirs and, then, sat down with his.

"Harry is one of our lawyers, Beynor," David said.

"Oh?" Beynor replied, suddenly very curious.

"Travis wants us to make you an offer for your shares in the corporation."

"I see," Beynor said.

"He misses you, you know," David said. "You could at least drop by, now and again. Even Steven says he sees very little of you anymore."

"I've good intentions," Beynor replied. While his relationship with Steven had gradually run its course, he knew he was keeping away from Travis for entirely different reasons.

"Do try to see Travis," David said. "Steven and I have never managed to get as close to him as you did."

How fortunate for you and Steven, Beynor thought.

"Right now, it's pretty hectic, what with the filming," Beynor alibied.

"I hear you're the next break-through male movie star on the horizon," David said.

"Don't believe everything you hear," Beynor replied, taking a large swallow of the liquor from his glass.

There was a moment of uneasy silence.

"So, Travis wants to buy me out, does he?" Beynor said finally.

"He's prepared to give you more than the shares are worth," David said. "That is, if you'll sell them."

Did Travis think he wouldn't?

"Why not sell?" he said with an indifferent shrug. He saw it as the ideal thing to do. It would be the cutting of the last strings that held him to Travis. Was that Travis's challenge: Either get away completely, or…?

Harry dug into his briefcase, coming out with several documents he spread out on the coffee table in front of them. Beynor glanced over the paperwork before signing it. Then, he took the certified check, whistled at the generous figure inscribed upon it. The lawyer tucked the signed papers back in his case and excused himself.

"How very quick and efficient that was," Beynor said, turning to David who still sat in the room. Beynor went to the dressing table and laid the check down, marveling at how final threads had finally been snipped.

"I suppose you wouldn't like to talk about what happened between you and Travis?" David asked.

"No."

"I still worry about him, Beynor. He's more moody since you abruptly pulled out of his life."

"I'm sorry," Beynor said. "I always liked him."

"But not sorry enough to go see him any time soon."

"It's the schedules," Beynor said, knowing that was a lie. "I never seem to be able to get away when he's free."

David finished his drink and stood. He walked to the door.

"Take care, Beynor," he said. "We do, *all* of us, miss you, you know?"

"What's that old bit about never being able to go home again?" Beynor said. "There's too much water under the bridge to go back, David. I'm not sure I even know for sure why I decided that the break had to be made, but it had to be made. Even Travis has apparently finally seen that."

"You think that's why he bought you out? To make the break a complete one?"

"You don't?"

"I don't know for sure," David said truthfully. "I somehow think a finalized break is the last thing he actually wants."

"Tell him hello for me, will you, David?" Beynor said, suddenly anxious to be alone. He had successfully managed to turn off his feelings toward Travis, up until now. He had no intentions of resurrecting those dead corpses at this late date.

"I will," David said, opening the door that led from the room.

Beynor watched the door shut. He went back to the bottle and poured himself a Scotch—a large one. Purposely, he'd not asked David if there had been any more beatings of gays by Travis that had been swept under the rug.

CHAPTER TWELVE

Beynor was wrong! It was *not* the same. Travis was a fool to have suspected that it might *ever* be the same. Travis let Reggie continue only because Travis's thoughts were lost in comparisons. He wondered how many of the attractive young men who had come into Reggie's presence, in this suite, had been subjected to Reggie's sick advances. Travis couldn't help imagining Beynor, stripped naked, in this very room, letting his body be touched by Reggie's exploring hands. Reggie had blown up several of the shots he had taken of Beynor from the original nude layout in *Before Dawn*. They were hung in prominent positions on the walls with several other poster-size photos of other hunky naked men.

Travis watched what Reggie was about, surprisingly detached. He wondered why he didn't just immediately stop this farce. He glanced back to Beynor's likenesses staring down at him from the walls. Travis shut his eyes, tried to bring back the way he had felt when he'd done with Beynor what he was now doing with Reggie.

Reggie had always known that, sooner or later, he would win. He had never been fooled, had always known that Travis could be brought around. No man, not even one who professed being the butchest around, was really averse to being serviced, if all they needed to do was stand there and let it happen. Reggie had known many a married straight man who had let him do what he was doing because their wives were too uptight to do it. Travis was no different. Look how passive he was.

Had Reggie known it was going to be this easy, he would have done it a long time ago. But he hadn't known it would be this easy. Reggie had always prided himself on being able to recognize the moment any potential was ripe for his approach. His intuition had really proved right on this day. Here he was, having sex with someone rumored to be unavailable to the gay population. Well, Reggie would certainly have tales to tell. Steven could go ahead and spread all the goddamned rumors he wanted about Travis's violent reaction to male sex. Reggie now knew better and admitted that he was a bit disappointed.

Travis wondered how Beynor did it. Travis had thought about that one particular facet of Beynor's character a lot since Beynor had decided to take his leave from the music environment. Travis thought about Beynor a lot, as a matter of fact. He thought he understood why Beynor had suddenly quit coming to the recording sessions, quit coming to the concerts, quit coming to the promotional and cocktail parties. Beynor had never made it a secret that he didn't want any emotional involvement. Travis could be flattered that Beynor so much feared that involvement in their particular instance that he had broken off all contact. Travis could be flattered, but that didn't help the inner churning in his guts. Beynor had given Travis something for which Travis had been searching his whole life. Beynor had allowed Travis a sampling and had, then, pulled it all way. Travis hadn't realized, when he trembled with Beynor into the void, that he would so miss the ecstasy after it was taken from him.

"Sex is sex is sex." That's what Beynor had cynically told Travis. Travis couldn't understand how that could be so. Travis found it ludicrous to even pretend that this man on his knees before him could conjure even half the pleasures that Beynor had been able to conjure.

"All sex can give you the desired orgasm." Travis thought he could hear Beynor muttering. As if to give credence to that subconscious echoing of his words, Beynor's pictures smiled down, knowingly, on the scene below.

In a way, Travis envied Beynor the ease with which the man could take his sex with another man. How much easier that must be than going through the ridiculous courtship of some woman.

Travis shut his eyes. He didn't want to see Beynor. Rather, he wanted to see Beynor but not as a one-dimensional form hanging on the wall. Travis wanted the whole man before him, wanted again the luxury of feeling that wondrous male flesh. Travis wondered if Beynor had known just how desperately Travis needed him. Perhaps it was the realization of the degree of desperation which had caused Beynor to decide to get away. How quickly he had managed his escape. How fast he had seized at the opportunity to break all his ties by taking up Travis's offer to buy his share of the existing corporation.

Travis shivered. He was letting Reggie take liberties that Travis had allowed no other homosexual, in that he still refused to admit Beynor was queer. Beynor was something else. He was someone who would service or be serviced by men but would not necessarily enjoy either. He used sex to get what he wanted. He hadn't used sex with Travis to get anything, though. He had cared for Travis in his own way, of that Travis was certain. Unfortunately, Beynor's way wasn't enough for Travis. Travis needed more. Was Reggie giving him more? Hell no!

Have a good time, Reggie, because there was going to be a price paid that Travis doubted very much the magazine man even had a clue.

Travis knew why he was here, allowing this degradation of his body. It was one more attempt for him to seek adjustment. After Beynor had left, it had been a long time before Travis felt the return of those profane desires inside him. That session with Beynor had left him completely drained. For the first time in ever so long, Travis had felt free, released of some horrible burden. He had hoped that burden was gone forever. It hadn't been. It came back, and, then, there was no longer a Beynor around to help him. Beynor had retired back into the safety of his own little world, again, indulging in meaningless sex as he climbed upward into another existence. Beynor was the new star of a movie that was rumored to be remaking movie history. His face was already appearing with some regularity in the entertainment magazines that Travis still managed to dominate as far as the printed word and the photographic images. Beynor had apparently been successful in shifting gears. He had found a formula for his living. Travis was looking for the formula to his own. Somehow, he doubted he would find it before it was too late.

Travis knew what he must do, knew it would someday come to this. He would only be fooling himself if he denied that he hadn't expected this moment. In a way, he had even prepared for it, protecting the only person he really cared for from the disaster resulting from what he must do. It didn't matter to him what happened to Steven or to David. Steven still would have more than enough money to cover his losses resulting from the collapse of the cult he had built around Travis. David? Travis had no sympathy for David. All that David had ever done had been to carve another place in the sun. He hadn't cared about Travis. The only one who had cared for Travis had been Beynor. Beynor had cared so much that he'd had to flee to safety. Travis could have gone after him, might have succeeded. He hadn't chanced it. He had no desire to destroy Beynor's world. It was better that Beynor get on in his.

Travis gazed down on Reggie, somehow sensing that the man actually knew what was coming and wouldn't make any move to stop it. It seemed almost as if Reggie wanted Travis to hit him, was waiting with both horror and anticipation for that very moment, and, in fact, had been waiting his whole miserable life, for Travis's hard fist to collide with flesh and hard bone. Travis felt bitter bile rising in his throat.

Travis's right hand doubled into a tight fist. It punched Reggie violently hard against the side of the head.

ABOUT THE AUTHOR

WILLIAM MALTESE, an international best-selling author of non-fiction and fiction articles, short stories, and novels, including his popular Wildside Mystery Double, *Incident at Aberlene* and *Incident at Brimzinsky* (Spies & Lies #1-#2), has published (under various pseudonyms) over 200 books in genres ranging from straight mainstream, to straight and gay erotica, as well as mystery, cozy mystery, romance, western, adventure, espionage, cooking, wine, young adult and children, plus twenty-four science fiction/fantasy'/horror novels, beginning with *Five Roads to Tlen* in 1969 (as "William J. Lambert III") through *Bond-Shattering* (2007). He's anything but a newcomer by way of fictionalized autobiographies and biographies, including his *Diary of a Hustler* (with "Joey"), *Slovakian Boy* (with "Pavel"), his shocking Lambda-Award-nominated Ardennian Boy (written with eminent gay scholar Professor Drewey Wayne Gunn) that raised more than a few eyebrows, while gleaning rave reviews, in its graphic portrayal of the scandalous literary and sexual relationship between the French poets Paul Verlaine and Arthur Rimbaud, and, most recently *Amen's Boy* (with Jacob Campbell) ripped from today's headlines and based on the scandalous tale of a young man who decides to become a Catholic priest but who, before he can graduate from seminary, must preserve his innocence from the physical mental, and sexual abuse of…a sadistic father, a violent brother, a molesting classmate, and a secret cabal of priests hiding within the very framework of Mother Church herself. For a comprehensive list of his literary output, See *Draqualian Silk: A Collector's and Bibliographical Guide to the Books of William Maltese*, 1969-2010 (Borgo Press, 2010). Maltese enlisted in the U.S. Army, where he achieved and was honorably discharged with the rank of Sergeant (E-5).

You can email him at: williammaltese@yahoo.com

www.ingramcontent.com/pod-product-compliance
Lightning Source LLC
Chambersburg PA
CBHW022049170626
46808CB00003B/1407